The Chronicles of Maximillian Fetterbrush

"You Might as Well Laugh About It"

And Laugh You Will!

By David Presnell

Disclaimer

This is a work of fiction. Names, characters, places, and incidents are the products of the author's imagination and/or are used fictitiously. Any resemblance to actual events, locales, or persons, living or dead, is entirely coincidental. The opinions expressed are those of the fictional characters and should not be confused with the authors.

Table of Contents

Introducing Maximillian Fetterbrush

In this book you will learn about the antics and life of a man named Maximillian Fetterbrush. Max, as we call him, is a person that has a little bit of all of us in him, and a person that we all desire to be a little more like, well, sometimes. At first thought, nobody really wants to be like Max, but it happens! As you get to know Max, you may find the secret to a happy life, if you look for it. For normal people, Max is the other side of the coin. For abnormal people, Max is probably their kinfolk. He might even be their daddy.

Teenagers love Max! Grandmas love Max! Most men "get" Max! Parents pray their teenagers won't be like Max! But Max causes everybody to laugh a little. He also teaches us that when life just doesn't go as planned, *you might as well laugh about it!*

In these chronicles, you will visit with Max on a day-to-day basis, not necessarily in that order, and you will share his adventures and comical ironies through Max's own eyes as he relives his experiences on paper. When things go bad for most people, they throw a fit and get depressed. When things go bad for Max, and they do quite often, he usually laughs about it and considers it a learning experience. His positive attitude will wear off on you too, if you will give him a chance. This book is a comical paradox and is destined to make you laugh your butt off so don't take it too seriously. Max wouldn't!

Hi! My name is David, the author. I suppose I'm Max's best, and possibly only real friend. I met Max many years ago at a small-town courthouse. As I heard him explain to the judge the reasons he was driving on the wrong side of the road, I looked up at the judge and realized the judge was believing every word Max was saying, and the cool thing was that Max was telling that judge the truth, but it was a truth that the judge "could believe". Max intrigued me so much that I got to know him, and I have kept in touch with him ever since. He loved to talk and tell his unique stories about his unbelievable and inspiring life.

I took notes and after a few years of encouraging him, he started writing his stories down on paper. His stories are not in any chronological order or on any timeline, and I present them to you in this book in the same order he presented them to me. When Max remembers some adventure, he writes it down. This book is a compilation of his stories that I put together for Max. I might be considered Max's personal unofficial editor, but my main job is to see that what Max writes gets to you, the reader, in its original form.

I suppose there are some things you need to know before you start reading about Max. If I don't explain these things, Max may not make any sense to you, and neither will this book. One important thing to keep in mind is that Max writes like he talks, and I am adamant about keeping Max's words pure Max. He talks a mix of deep Louisiana Southern and North Carolina Blue Ridge Mountain slang. Sometimes he talks and writes like a college professor, and sometimes he talks like a hillbilly. It all depends on the mood he's in. If you don't know Max, his talking might seem to be strange, at first. However, as Max puts it, *"Getting through to other people's brains is what's important, not fancy talking!"* It is my desire to present Max as Max, not some doctored up version of Max. When Max says or writes "y'all" he means "y'all" not "you all" and that's exactly how he writes it. He doesn't use any special punctuation to indicate a word is slang because to Max, it's not slang. It's communication and to us it's funny. Max will teach you how to get over bad days, lighten up a little, and laugh a lot. Life's too short to be so serious!

Max is not stupid or ignorant, in fact, he is very intelligent, informed, and wise. He believes that just because someone is book smart doesn't necessarily mean that they are intelligent, especially if they have very little real-life experience. Max has a lot of real-life experience. Max reads books all the time and considers reading a way to learn about life all over the world, but life experience is what Max is really all about. Max is what I call a mystery or a conundrum or an enigma. At first glance some people may call Max a bum or hobo. Max lives life somewhat like a hobo, but Max is the total opposite of a bum or hobo. Max does not have a lazy bone in his body. He just knows how to take life easy and use his brain more than his muscles. Max only works when he needs money. Max can walk into any town in America and within an hour have enough money, earned through his intelligence (slick thinking) and from gainful employment, to buy food and enough gas to fill up his moped and his carry-on gas can.

Yeah, Max is a moped man. He believes automobiles, televisions, computers, cell phones, and many other modern gadgets speed life up way too much and takes away our freedom by taking away our free time. He believes seeing the world should be by foot or "ped" as he calls his moped. Some may ask, "Does Max drink or smoke or do drugs or believe in God?" I'm sure Max dabbles, but I can tell you this; I have never seen Max falling down drunk or wasted on drugs. I know he doesn't smoke cigarettes because he says they are too costly. As far as God is concerned, I have seen Max do what I think is his version of praying and talking to God. He doesn't push his beliefs on anyone, and that's another reason I like him. Yeah, Max is a God-fearing man! I have never seen Max judge another person for their bad habits either. Many times, I have heard Max say something to the effect of, *"All of us have our problems! No need for me to add to them by judging someone else! I guess I need to look in the mirror when I get that desire to judge someone!"*

Max is a practicing herbalist. Some people might even call him a spiritualist or healer. Max studies the medicinal and edible value of wild plants, herbs, shrubs, and trees, and will quickly tell you that he believes that God has placed everything you need in the form of food and medicine right around you and this includes everything God has made and pretty much nothing man has made. I know there has been times that Max visited medical doctors, but he doesn't go often. He says it's just too costly and, in most cases, he gripes that they did him more harm than good.

I know Max was born on the Mississippi River in the great state of Louisiana. I'm not sure of the town and I don't think Max really knows either. He has moved around a lot and ended up in the Blue Ridge Mountains of North Carolina in his younger years. He tells you about some of this in his stories. Max eats when he's hungry, sleeps when he's tired, goes when there is somewhere to go, and talks when he needs to talk whether anyone is listening or not. Max doesn't like to fight but if pushed, he'll take on a nest of hornets or a gang of punks and consider it fun. No, he doesn't always win his battles, but he always just patches up his wounds as best he can and laughs about it when it's all over.

One of his famous statements is, *"You might as well laugh about it, especially if you can't change it!"* Max studies and thinks a lot about a lot of things. He can fix just about anything that's broke if he has the tools and parts available. He fixes people quite often too, from broken hearts to people that are caught up in their depressing lives and cannot seem to find any reasons for it all. Max can lift people out of depression better than anyone I have ever seen. Max seems to have figured out the reason God put us here, at least for him. I think that is another reason I like hanging around Max. He always makes me feel good about myself and my life. Max prefers love over hate and Max has never been very picky about the women he falls in love with. He says, *"All women need loving… little women, big women, short women, tall women and so on! I'll date a rich woman, but poor girls are more faithful, far more fun, and much easier to please!"* Yes, Max is a lady's man!

Some people ask me if Max is a real person. That makes me laugh. Max is the person many of us would like to be. When you're ready, you can read this book

and think about it, but only if you want to! Now, you could put yourself in Max's shoes for a little while! Relax, dream, laugh a little, and let Max take your imagination on a few journeys that you may have never been on before, and as Max says, "Enjoy!"
David Presnell, Author

Episode One: Fast Food

Back when I was young and recently married, I remember the event with my new little wife Jenny and her four kids that pretty much ended my first marriage. I had made the mistake of asking my new little family if they would like something from the fast-food place in town. It was a twelve-mile trip, and it was late on a Saturday evening, but after all, it was my honeymoon. Jenny and I had gone to the justice of the peace early that morning and got hitched. I took her and her kids back to the trailer where we worked the rest of the day, mowing, trimming, and washing clothes, and all the other typical summer Saturday family duties, except that this day was one of those that lasted late into the evening. Everyone was exhausted and hungry.

I got up off the couch and took their orders, carefully having Jenny write everything down, and off I headed to town all by myself. This was before cell phones and laptops and the drive-thru seemed to be the fastest way to get my new family fed. No one wanted to go with me but rather stay and get cleaned up. My theory was that there was something they wanted to see on TV. (This was before VCR's too, I believe).

When I arrived at that drive-thru about 7 pm, there were about seven or eight cars in line. As I slowly moved the old Dodge Dart through the line (it was my new wife's old car), I reached the point of no return. This is the point in line where they block you in with cement and shrubs. No pulling out of line now. When I finally reached the order window, the kind voice behind the speaker box carefully stated, *"What can I get for you?"* I reached for the list in my pocket and guess what? That list didn't make it to town. I searched all my pockets and seat to be sure, but no list. Cars were lining up for some distance behind me.

The voice more firmly stated: *"Can I help you?"* "Ah… yeah… ah … I, thinking to myself - let's see Billy doesn't eat hamburgers, Johnny loves hamburgers, Sally is a vegetarian I think, Jill - I can't remember, and my wife will eat whatever I get her." *"Do you want to place an order or what?"* "Yes, I would like a fish sandwich for Billy, a super burger for Johnny, a large salad for Sally, and for Jill I guess another fish sandwich. Oh, and a large hamburger for my wife." (That wasn't so hard).

"Sir, was that second item with or without cheese?" "With, I guess!" (Horns were now blowing behind me). "Would you like your fish grilled or breaded sir?" "Oh, I don't know - just choose one!"

"Sir, would you like your fish sandwiches grilled or breaded?" "Grilled will be fine!"

"On that large hamburger sir, would you like cheese on it?" "Sure, why not!" "Would you like to make these combos, sir?" "No, I guess not." "Sir, it's only one dollar more and you basically get your drink free. Are you sure you don't what to make these combos?" "Ok - Sure! Make them combos." "Sir, you can giant size these for only 39 cents per meal. Would you like to giant size these, sir?" "Absolutely! Make them big!" "OK sir, what would you like to drink with these?" "The first thing the cups come in contact with will be fine, madam!" "You don't have to be hateful, sir. What would you like to drink with these?" (I had been thinking.) "I want Cokes® for everybody." "I'm sorry sir, we only sell Pepsi® products." "Pepsi's® for everybody." "That will be $28.65, sir. Please pull around." It occurred to me I had forgotten myself. I waited, tooted the horn, and finally her sweet voice came back on the speaker. "Can I do something else for you sir?" "I forgot myself. Just give me a number one meal with a Pepsi® and make it a giant size." How's that?" "Please pull around for your total sir." "Thank you!"

Cars were lined up back into the main highway and people were getting ill. You could tell the place was understaffed and overworked. Finally, I'm almost to the window and I reach for my wallet. As I pull up to the window with wallet in hand, the girl states, *"That will be $39.15 sir."* As I open my wallet, I see a beautiful new-looking ten dollar bill all by itself. I had forgotten that I had to pay $10 for our marriage license and $20 for the justice of the peace. I ask, "Ah, do you all take checks?" (This was before ATM machines, too.) "I only have $10.00. I can write a check for the rest. Can you just ask the manager, please?" *"You will have to come inside sir."* After some smooth talking I convinced the manager to cash a personal check for me for the difference.

Once I got all the food into the Dodge, including the six half-gallon cups of super-size drinks, I realized the shopping bag full of food could sit in the floor of the passenger side, but where do I put these top-heavy drinks? I set them strategically around in the back floorboard and back seat.

Some idiot pulled out in front of me as I was leaving the parking lot. I had to slam on the brakes. I noticed brown foaming liquid flowing up around the gas pedal. Oh well, I can drink water. When I finally arrived home, three of the drinks were actually still in the cups and everyone was screaming "We're starving - where have you been?" Without talking I handed them the shopping bag full of wholesome, nutritious food.

Then the griping and complaining started. "I hate fish! I'm allergic to fish! I never get cheese on a burger! Where is the salad dressing? Honey, there's only enough sandwiches in here for four people, and I think there is eight orders of fries." I decided to walk to the local gas station and pick up a loaf of bread and some bologna. A little mustard and I will have supper. I went in, got my bread and sandwich meat (he actually had a pack of boiled ham in the cooler), and proceeded to the checkout where a large sign stated, "We do not take checks!" After begging and pleading the owner finally accepted my check for $9.63.

When I got back home, I piled on the meat, cheese, and mustard, sat down and started to take a big bite and I noticed a soured smell from the boiled ham and something green on the bread. Yep, the ham was spoiled, and the bread was molded! It was all fine since I had the trailer all to myself. There was a note on the fridge, telling me that they were going home to Jenny's mother's house and that they never wanted to see me again. Sure enough, the old Dodge Dart was gone. So glad that's over! My first marriage lasted about 18 hours.

Episode Two: The Moped

The soaring gas prices bring back many memories of my teenage years. I remember back in the early seventies when gasoline went from 24¢ per gallon to 99¢ per gallon in just a few months. This was long before I moved to the Blue Ridge Mountains. I remember waiting in long lines only to be allowed to buy three gallons of gas. I remember the oil embargo, the Iran hostage crisis, and double-digit inflation. I also remember the many ways people tried to save money on the price of fuel.

One new item that found its way to my town was a motorized bike with pedals, otherwise known as a moped. The early mopeds were funny looking contraptions with small motors and large pedals unlike the nice sleek powerful scooters of today. As long as you were on level ground or going downhill, the bikes were good for about 25 miles per hour. When you started going uphill you always had to start pedaling to make it up the hill. You could also buy small motors for the front wheel of your bicycle from the Sears & Roebuck® catalog. I chose the classic moped for my gas-saving teen years. It was well used when I acquired it. I think it had been in several crashes. Here are some of my early experiences with my seventies moped.

The guy at the moped dealership (they called him "Dealing Johnny" - who also sold used cars) told me it was used but would still get at least 125 miles per gallon. He was right, too. The best I remember, to get this thing going you turned on the fuel, primed the carburetor, turned on the switch, and started pedaling until the motor started and kept the throttle on the handlebar rolled on wide open. I remember wobbling a lot. These things were very hard to balance since they moved so slowly and were much heavier than a traditional bicycle. I suppose that I had to have it, so I swapped my 1963 Chevrolet in for a brand new (well, almost new) moped. Looking back, I guess things had to be learned the hard way. Of course, I only paid $100 for that old junk Chevy. It was pretty much shot but it did make it to Dealing Johnny's lot. I didn't have a clear title to the Chevy, but Johnny worked all that out. He didn't have a clear title to the moped either, so it was all good.

In those days, there were no motorcycle safety training programs or other requirements for mopeds or motorcycles. You just cranked it on, pedaled the thing, and hopefully, off into the sunset you went. The first real challenge was to get the thing off the parking lot and have all the people at the dealership see how cool a biker I was, being a regular viewer of "*Then Came Bronson*". I got out of the parking lot just in the nick of time. That truck was really going fast. I pedaled and rode until I finally made my first stop at the neighborhood gas station. I remember the look on the attendant's face when I handed him fifteen cents for my gas and told him to keep the change. Ha! I'll whip these high fuel prices into submission!

As I pedaled on home, I noticed how that every time you hit a hole or bump the rear wheel seemed to bounce right off the ground. I do not remember this machine having much in the way of shock absorbers (or power) at least on the rear. It was a slow bumpy ride, but I was saving at least three dollars a week on gas. Since my first wife Jenny had left, I was now an available man. The money I saved would now allow me to ask my sweetheart from high school, Natalia Pendergras for her hand in marriage. (She could now become Mrs. Natalia Fetterbrush, the wife of the man who had whipped high gas prices into submission). These were all fine thoughts that were going through my mind on my ten-mile, hour-long trip home from the moped dealer.

When I arrived home, (I was now living with my parents since I was thrown out of the trailer park where Jenny and I honeymooned), my dad asked me, with little interest in my new (used) moped where my Chevy was. Oh well, he'll come around. I was a bit sore from the ride home, but I had to call Natalia and tell her the good news. "Honey, with my job at the grocery store and my new bike, well, I wanted to ask you in person, but I just can't wait. Natalia, will you marry me?" She said, "Yes!" Didn't take her long either. I was proud. She wanted to ride my new motor bike. That's what she called it, at first, anyway. I remember her rambling on something about going to California for our honeymoon on our new motor bike. Oh well; she can work out all the details. I just agreed to show up to the wedding. I was lying awake all night thinking about marrying Natalia and my new (almost new) moped. It was a good time in my life, at least that night.

The next day, I discussed the marriage plans with my parents, who had all sorts of questions and negatives such as, "What happened to you and Jenny?" "What will you do to provide for her?" "Where will you live?" "How will you get around"? Ah! My new moped will get us around just fine. I can ride to work and back for about $1.00 a week. They started throwing around silly questions such as, "How will you get groceries home"? Any real biker knows what a milk crate and bungee strap are made for. I may even get a tattoo.

When I arrived at Natalia's house, she was looking beautiful as she ran to open the door. "You have to ask Daddy," were the words that came from her mouth as she passed me by and ran out to the curb where my motor bike was parked. "It's cool!" she exclaimed. She had told her mom about me asking her to marry me, and Mom, who promised not to tell Dad, had told Dad; and I walked right into the room where Dad was sitting with a look that could have turned diamonds back into coal.

I didn't have enough life experience or common sense at that date in time to really know how little my life was really worth to her daddy at that moment. "Got something to say to me - boy?" My big dumb grin turned into pure fear and trembling. I suddenly realized her dad wanted to kill me. He was a really big man. That's where Natalia got her extra pounds from. Her beauty made up for her slightly over 263-pound body. She was real short, too. That made her look bigger than she really was. I loved every pound of that girl.

"Mr. Pendergras, sir, I would like to ask you for your beautiful daughter's hand in marriage. Natalia and I have decided to get married this weekend by the justice of the peace in town." I remember hearing her mom dreadfully exclaiming in the back of the room, "Oh my lord, she's pregnant!" "I can assure you, Mrs. Pendergras, that we have never done anything other than hold hands and kiss!!" "Shut up, boy," stated Dad.

"Just exactly why do you want to marry our little Nat Nat?" "I love her, sir!" After answering questions similar to those posed by my dad and mom, Mr. Pendergras asked me how much I made at that grocery store. I proudly told him, "I make $1.60 per hour, sir, and have worked my way up to head bagboy and assistant produce manager. I'm getting over 24 hours per week now." "You don't even have a decent car," exclaimed Mrs. Pendergras. "I got rid of that old Chevy!" I went on to explain about my new (used) moped and how much money I will save. The moped idea did not go over well at all, but Natalia came in about this time and smoothed everything out with Dad and Mom. She was an only child and usually got just exactly what she wanted, and she wanted me (and my new used motor bike).

I took Natalia on her first ride later that evening. I had not read the little instruction book that came with the moped. I figured that little machine had a weight limit, but I wasn't sure what it was. Together, Natalia and I were pushing close to 400 pounds. I just put a little more air in the tires, and she did fine (the moped that is). With the two of us, top speed seemed to be around 15 miles per hour on level ground. I did have my first mishap that evening. I wore these black heavy-duty, steel-toed military boots. Some called them logger boots, but they looked real cool on my moped. Anyway, not more than 100 yards from Natalia's house as I started up a hill pedaling faster, Natalia slid forward to keep from falling off that small seat. As my foot went around, I kicked her right in the shin... hard!

After wobbling to a stop, I got off and was trying to help her off without her falling, but she, whining and crying about me kicking her, got her foot caught on something as she threw it over the seat and down she went. I grabbed her shoulder and the bike's handlebar. It was too late. Natalia hit the pavement skinning her hands and arms a bit and the bike hit the pavement breaking off one of the signal lights. Oh well, I could use hand signals, at least until after we were married.

The day of the wedding, I washed and waxed that moped. I was proud. I had purchased a bottle of something I had never used before called ArmorAll®. It made the tires, seats, and just about anything that was not metal real shiny. My moped looked sharp.

I learned several things that day. ArmorAll® is a fine product, but you do not put it on moped or motorcycle tires, and you do not put it on a seat which will be occupied by a big bride with a tight, slick as silk, wedding dress, and you certainly do not put it on the handgrips of the handlebar of a Moped. But that's not all I learned!

The wedding was uneventful (at least at first). Her parents and mine showed up as witnesses and the justice of the peace was real friendly. He asked about Jenny and I just pretended I didn't hear him. He asked for his money up front. Forgot about that! I had put my last bit of cash into the items I had purchased to shine up my moped. As I stood beside my Natalia during the ceremony, I could see her (my moped) out of the corner of my eye sitting on the front lawn of that courthouse. My parents looked at her parents. My mom said something about it being the bride's family that pays for the wedding. Natalia's mom pulled out the $20.00 fee for the justice of the peace and the $10.00 marriage license fee and the wedding proceeded.

Natalia had on a real old hand-me-down wedding dress. It was beautiful and almost fit her. Her mom found it at a piece goods shop where they sold used wedding gowns for $5.00. Sounds like a bargain to me.

Natalia and I walked out as Mr. and Mrs. Maximillian Fetterbrush. The justice of the peace and our parents threw rice. We climbed on our new (used) moped and I proceeded to start pedaling off that courthouse lawn into the street. I told her to hold on real tight. I bounced over the small curb onto the pavement with no problem and that little engine was running real fine now.

Natalia let one hand go from around my waist to wave bye to everyone and I hit a pothole or manhole cover or something. I heard a thump and some screaming, and my moped went completely out of control I think due to the ArmorAll® on the tires, but I managed to recover and keep her from crashing. My moped had really nice big mirrors. It was hard to tell with all the wedding dress pieces blowing around, but I believe my dear Natalia was sitting flat on her behind in the middle of the street. I guess that dress was so tight that she didn't have on much under it, and most of her dress was still attached to my moped somehow.

After all the fuss was over, Natalia was alright, just bruised a little. I thought her dad and my dad were going to come to blows over some comment her dad made about the intelligence of our family. Her mom & dad took her home where she put on real biker clothes.

I picked her up and off we went on our honeymoon. We didn't really have any plans, just rode around for a while and went back to my home. I did want to take her to the new fast-food restaurant in town. It had the first drive-thru and we were going to get our food and take it over to the park and eat. Yes, it's the same one that caused mine and Jenny's divorce.

There was a long line. We ordered the burger meals with fries and drinks and continued to sit in line. That was cool because everyone in town was admiring my new (used) moped. When we got up to the window, the boy told me it would be $9.10. He was a good friend and I told him about us just getting married. He told me he had heard, and that he had also heard how I had almost killed the bride. As I opened my wallet, I asked him if he had ever used ArmorAll®. "Sure, I use it all the time," he answered. "Just don't put it on the steering wheel or seat. It'll make it real slick." Uh-huh!

As my billfold opened up, I realized that I didn't have a dime to my name; spent it all on shining stuff for my moped. After pleading with my friend at the drive-thru, he told me he would pay for it, and I could pay him back on payday. What a friend! He handed us the bag and two drinks. I told Natalia to hold on to the seat real tight with her knees, hold a drink in each hand, and set the bag between us. I didn't have time to purchase a milk crate for the luggage rack yet, and it was only a mile to the park.

We eased out of the parking lot and made it onto the main road. I managed to get her up to top speed in town. Everybody was eyeing my new (used) moped. We made it to the only red light in town and came to a stop. When the light changed, someone yelled and tooted their horn. They knew we were just married. I wanted to impress them, so I rolled on the gas for a quick takeoff. You know that ArmorAll® lasts a long time.

I remember one of the Coke® cups hitting me upside my head as dear Natalia slid right off the back of my moped. She got up and had something like a fit; told me she never wanted to see me again and got into a car with one of her friends who was at the scene. (In those days everyone hung out in town). Part of one of the burgers and some of the fries were still intact, so I managed to stuff some of them down my shirt and pedal on to the park where I could eat in peace. I guess the street sweeper will get the rest. I finally got to look at the owner's manual. The first page said in big bold letters: **"Warning: Not Designed for Two Riders!"** Hmm… Imagine that!

Natalia's parents got something called an annulment to get me out of the marriage. It's probably for the best since I wasn't really divorced from Jenny anyway. Those moped years were really great. It's been many years ago, but I'm thinking about getting me a new one to save gas. Everybody's selling them and they are much nicer than the old machines.

Episode Three: The Camping Trip

Before I finally gave up on staying married, keeping a job, owning a car or a house, I used to take the current family camping every year. I remember one year in particular. I had just purchased a new 1987 Geo Tracker 4-wheel drive with 60 months of payments and everything that goes with it. It was the hardtop version with a cool luggage rack on top. I thought it would be a perfect family car as long as we left most of the kids at home. We had owned it a couple of weeks when I had the bright idea of taking the little lady and a couple of the kids on a 4-wheel drive camping trip up in the National Forest - a place where I could "lock in those hubs". The boys wanted to stay home (so did the girls, but they were smaller than the boys and would all fit in the back of my new 4-wheel drive). I started packing gear about 7 am on Saturday morning. Couldn't wait to hit the road! By 3 pm, I almost had everything packed. That luggage rack was really great. I had all the gear packed on top with some snack food and other necessities in the back behind the girls.

After much encouragement (and a few arguments), I finally got everyone away from the TV and loaded into that Tracker. You wouldn't believe how much junk those girls wanted me to take camping, and you wouldn't believe how much weight one of those vehicles would hold. I quietly went through the so-called necessities that the girls were tossing to me from the deck, and the things I didn't see as necessities, I carefully hid in the basement. They would never miss their makeup kits and other junk. Who in their right mind brings a hair dryer to the great outdoors? I was really tired from packing everyone's stuff, but, finally, we were on our way. We started up the road like a boat in water. That Tracker was really overloaded, but she was handling well enough. What was that? Something made a loud noise. I didn't dare back off that gas as we were starting to make speed up the hill. I looked in the mirror. Yep! It was one of my large sticks of split hardwood I had strategically lashed on top for the evening fire. There would be plenty of firewood up there off the forest road anyway. Hope no one hits that log laying in the road. It was about 4 pm now on a nice, almost perfectly clear, early September evening.

Once I got to town, I stopped at a gas station to put some more air in those tires. The back ones were really mushroomed out with all the weight and everything. I noticed some people laughing as we made our way out of town toward the High-Country

Wilderness. I suppose they thought it funny that I covered all the gear on top with a big orange tarp. All that valuable gear had to be kept dry in the event of a shower. Of course, the weather service had sealed this trip with their promise that it was going to be clear for the next four days, but I covered it all up just in case. That bundle of gear was almost as high on top as the vehicle itself. We made it to the state line just before 5 pm. It was hours before dark.

My sweet wife said, "There must be a wreck up ahead; there's cops everywhere." It wasn't a wreck. It was a roadblock. Must be looking for an escaped convict or something. As I pulled up, I noticed one of the officers bent over laughing. They must have been telling some good jokes between cars. As we pulled closer, a nicely dressed officer said 'hello' and asked to see my driver's license and registration. I handed him my license and explained that I had just purchased the vehicle and had not received the registration yet. He asked to see the bill of sale. I asked my dear wife where it was and she quickly told me, "I don't know where it is, nor do I care." "Sir, I think I left it on the kitchen table. You can call the dealer if they are still open." One of my sweet wife's daughters made some wisecrack that the officer did not like. The officer told me to pull over to the shoulder and for everybody to get out of the vehicle.

It turned out they were looking for a stolen white vehicle. Oh, well. Ours was certainly white. They looked over the vehicle and while they were waiting for the dispatcher to verify me being the owner of the vehicle, they wanted to look under that orange tarp. I guess they thought it could be a ton of dope or something, since I was going out of the way to try to hide it under that bright orange tarp. I proceeded to loosen the bailing twine ropes I had tied to the front and back bumpers so we could raise up an edge of the tarp. Once the officers saw all the high-tech camping gear, they nicely told me I could reattach the rope. They were super nice. As I started tying everything back up to the bumpers, they got a call on the radio that I was not a mad killer or car thief and that I could go. I quickly finished tying off the tarp, we loaded up, and with a "be careful" from the officers, we proceeded on our way up into the High Country for our wilderness adventure. It was about 6:30 pm now, but we only had about 40 miles of travel until we hit the forest road. It was about 12 miles up the dirt forest road to the campsite I had planned on.

We finally arrived at the entrance of the National Forest and started up the rough dirt road to the wilderness camping area. I was really moving on over rocks and the steep and narrow terrain of forest road. I stopped just long enough to lock in the front hubs.

Man, I was 4-wheeling now. I had her up to 20 mph in the straights. I wanted to get to that campsite before dark. I got to a narrow curve with a huge cliff on one side, a bank on the other side, and big Ford Truck coming straight at me. I locked her down and stopped just short of his bumper. I heard one of the girls say, "Cool." This machine had really good brakes. My dear wife had other things to say, but we backed up and found a place to pass. All was well.

We finally made it to the campsite. This was one of those National Forest Wilderness spots that just had a pull-off and a flat area for the tent and a homemade rock fireplace. This was a real 4-wheel drive campsite with no picnic tables, no bathrooms, no electricity, no running water, no TV's, just peace and… just quiet.

As we pulled in, the automatic headlights turned on. It was basically dark. As I opened the door, I noticed one of the twine ropes was loose from the tarp. The tarp had apparently been flapping in the wind for some time. I guess it didn't get tied back on good at the road check. I could not find a flashlight. It was packed on the bundle on top, too. I wasn't expecting to arrive after dark. I noticed the bundle was loose, too, and it seemed some of the gear was missing. Oh well, we'll just rough it.

I proceeded to get what was left of the stuff off onto the ground. The girls, including my sweetie, would not get out of the vehicle. They were mumbling something about bears, going home, stupid camping trip, and divorce. I got some junk food and warm drinks out of the back and tossed some up front to see if that would shut everyone up. Yeah, I forgot to get ice at the station. No big deal! Warm soda had to be good for us! It'll make you burp. I realized that the tent, lawn chairs, sleeping bags, and most of the good food was gone. No big deal! We'll peel some bark if we eat up all the corn cheese. There was plenty of junk food, especially my favorite, red hot pork rinds and potted meat. That could almost be considered survival food.

I got the gas lamp started (it was hanging on to one of the luggage rack's rails) and proceeded to build a fire, and for a city boy, I was pretty good at it. I still had a few large sticks of firewood left on top. In fact, they were what was holding down most of the junk still up there. There was plenty of drinks and water. Most of them were in the big ice chest behind the girls' seat. Wished I had remembered the ice! Oh, well. With the fire roaring, the girls and my sweetie finally removed themselves from the Tracker. "Where are the chairs?" "They didn't make it!" "Where's our sleeping bags?" "They didn't make it either!" "It's a good thing it is a clear night." We were high up in the mountains. The temperature was dropping, and the wind was really howling now. Just as I made that statement about it being a clear night, it started to rain hard. That is about when the Federal Ranger came by and politely informed me that a fire ban was on in the wilderness, motor vehicles were not allowed where I was parked, and there was no camping allowed here. "We're not camping!" I exclaimed. "We don't even have a tent or sleeping bags." He wrote me three tickets for my illegal activities and one for littering. (Apparently some of my items had fallen out along the road on the way up. They called it littering.) I think it cost me about $3,000 (or 6-months – yeah, I took the 6-months – didn't have $3,000) to get out of those tickets. Oh, well.

After threats of divorce and hurtful things happening to me in the middle of the night, the girls and my sweetie locked themselves in the Tracker, and they had the keys and were threatening to use them. I knew when I was beat. "Let's go home!"

On our way home, I had to stop and change a tire. Apparently, my camping spot had leftover nails where some good ol' boys had been burning boards with nails in them many years earlier. The Tracker was very easy to change a tire on, even at 1 am. Everybody calmed down after we got back home. At least I finally got my peace and quiet. No one was speaking to me. It was interesting that a few weeks after that trip, I read an ad in the classified section of a local trading paper that read: "For Sale: Large tent, four sleeping bags including one large man's oversize cold weather bag, four heavy-duty lawn chairs, one two-burner camp stove, four cans propane, one inflatable king-size camp bed, many small supplies including a battery operated TV, radio, battery operated hair dryer, and many other items too numerous to mention. It occurred to me that those girls had gotten wise to me hiding junk in the basement and slipped it back in under that tarp anyway. Good enough for them. I had to go and see if I could buy my junk back, at a decent price, (or steal it back) from the person who had found it. I traded some old tires and rims to my cousin Pete for all that camping gear anyway. He probably stole all that stuff from somebody else.

Episode Four: A Fishing Trip

Thinking about my experiences of my younger days on my Moped and camping trips, also brings to mind my first fishing trip to the Blue Ridge Mountains. My family moved around a lot, but I think I was married, living in a small town near the Mississippi River, when my friend Joe talked me into the idea of going trout fishing in the mountains of North Carolina. Joe had just returned from one of his Blue Ridge Mountain adventures and he was set and determined to go back in a week before the season closed. In those days, trout season didn't last all year. Joe was also set and determined to have me go with him. After thinking about it for a moment, my current wife at that time was Roxanne, and we already had one child on the way, and she wasn't very happy about me wanting to go fishing. I never really believed that kid was mine, but that's another story. I had to do some begging and pleading, but she agreed to let me go with Joe for a week to catch trout… not just any trout… rainbow trout from the Blue Ridge Mountains.

I set out to the local sporting goods store and asked them what I would need to catch rainbow trout in the rivers and creeks of the Blue Ridge and explained that we were leaving at 4 am in the morning for the all-day drive to the mountains. I also explained how I would need some camping gear. Joe told me not to buy anything; that he had all the equipment I needed except for a sleeping bag, but I did not want to go empty-handed on my first trip. The fine man at the sporting goods store proceeded to explain that their store primarily carried gear for fishing and camping in the Mississippi River area, but he thought he could "help me out of a jam". Fishing and camping on the Mississippi was never a big deal. It was always warm, and you could sleep on the riverbank most of the time without any fancy gear. The Blue Ridge Mountains of North Carolina was really different from the banks of the Mississippi. I left that store with almost $500 worth of trout fishing equipment and camping gear. Them must be tough fish, them rainbow trout from the Blue Ridge Mountains.

I met Joe at his house at 3 am the next day. Joe laughed at me for buying all that gear (junk as he called it), but he helped me pack my gear into the back of his 1976 Ford Ranger pickup anyway. It had a camper shell on it, but there was so much junk in the back of that truck, it was unlikely that we would be spending the night in it. Joe had planned to camp a few nights and stay a night or two at an area motel, explaining that the camping would save us some money, and give us direct access to the great outdoors. We left right on time. Joe liked to be on time. At 4 am on what I remember to be a Thursday morning, I was on the trip of a lifetime. I was on my way to the Blue Ridge Mountains to catch trout.

On our long trip up, Joe explained to me all the different types of trout that we might catch. In those days, most of the trout waters in the mountains were stocked regularly with rainbow and brown trout. Brook or native trout were commonly available, and at that time were self-supporting in most of the streams and rivers in the mountains. Joe told me about all the many ways you could catch trout and about the gear he used. He told me about hip and chest waders and fly rods, his favorite handmade fly, and many other cool tools necessary to bring down them powerful mountain trout. After several stops, we finally arrived at a private campground in the center of the beautiful Blue Ridge Mountains with stocked trout streams running nearby. The owners of the campground all new Joe by name. I was beginning to get excited. It was still daylight and Joe wanted to "get a hook wet", as he called it. I did to.

The camp host told us about his favorite nearby stream, so we headed there first. After trying out my new fly rod for the first time, I decided that overhanging brush and fly-fishing just did not go together. Joe got pretty mad at me beating, cussing, and thrashing around in the water. I finally just dropped the hook into the water and let it float downstream. Suddenly, after hours of nothing, I felt a nibble, then a hit. My pole starting bending. Lord, I had a fish. I jumped, pulled, reeled, and with much advice from Joe, I got that fish out of the creek. It was a pretty rainbow trout at least a foot long. Boy, she was pretty.

About that time, a nice gentleman with an official-looking uniform approached us and asked to see our licenses. Hmm, forgot about that. Joe had his, and as he tried to explain that we had driven all day and had forgotten about getting my license, the officer asked to see our fish. He was really nice. "If I could keep my catch, it would still be worth the fine," I thought. Well, it turns out my foot-long trout was only about six inches. After he threatened to arrest me, he started to write me a ticket for fishing without a license and keeping under length fish. Joe had to open his big mouth with something about the police picking on people from Louisiana ("F" word included many times). I tried to get him to shut up, but it was too late. You see, Joe was a leftover hippy from the sixties who had quit smoking pot and learned to fish for the calming effect it had on him. As the wildlife officer proceeded to call for backup (Joe was cussing and threatening him with violence now), I was fearing for my life.

The officer, with his hand on his pistol, proceeded to place us both under arrest and with handcuffs in place, started to search Joe's truck. You know, only Joe could have had the wisdom to hide an AK-47 Assault Rifle behind the seat of his truck - fully loaded with a 30-round clip to help catch fish. I don't have a clue why he had four sticks of dynamite in a box in the back of that truck, either. I think he said something to the officer about using them to catch fish with ("F" word included many times). Oh well! The first night in jail was really nice. When we arrived, everyone in the jail was telling Joe that it was good to see him again, and that they were glad to have him back. Hmm! There was this sweet little lady who cooked the jail's food, and it was truly some of the best country cooking I had ever eaten. I never saw my prized six-inch trout again. I hoped it might be served to me for supper, considering what trouble it caused, but it never happened. I brushed up on my tattooing skills and artistic plastic spoon-twisting while in jail in the Blue Ridge Mountains. My first call was to my dear wife. That didn't go over well at all. As bad as it all seemed, it turned out that at our hearing, Joe apologized, I apologized, the gun checked out as legal, the dynamite magically disappeared (I think that officer needed some better fishing gear than what he'd been using) and after a few fines and warnings, we were on our way back to some good rainbow trout fishing.

We ended up making friends with the arresting officer, and he told us a really great place to find the best rainbow trout in the county. My trout was truly over 14 inches and cooked up perfectly. After dining at that fine country seafood restaurant in town, we started on our long journey home. That's right, we never made it back to the creek. Joe was mad at me. He blamed it all on my stupidity of not getting a license. I asked him how he was so well-known at that jail, but he never answered. I think he loved the attention and the food. I felt something special in those mountains that I had never felt before. Joe liked visiting those mountains, but there was something that came over me there. I wanted to live there! I don't know why, but I knew that sometime in the future I would become a mountain man.

When we arrived back in the Louisiana Bayou country to the place I called home, my dear Roxanne had thrown all my stuff (anything she could not pawn for cash) out into the street with a note for me to do certain things. I can't repeat them here, but they implied that she no longer wanted to be my wife. In fact, over the two weeks I had been fishing (well, serving time), she had moved her friend from work into our house. He was much bigger and meaner than me. I was a certified criminal now, but I just didn't have the heart to fight. I had just been beaten down, arrested, and thrown in jail because of a six-inch rainbow trout from the Blue Ridge Mountains. How could I go up against a big powerful man like Joe's big brother Jim? He deserved Roxanne. I noticed he favored (as in looked like) her kids more than me, too. Oh, well!

It occurred to me that it must be God's will for me to be in the Blue Ridge Mountains. I loaded my stuff in the back of Joe's truck, (he felt sorry for me since my wife had moved his brother in) and had him haul me back to the mountains of North Carolina. I was on my way to becoming a mountain man. I had no idea what was ahead, and I had no idea that Joe had slipped a stick of dynamite with cap and fuse into one of my bags with a note attached that said, "Hope you catch a big one."

Episode Five: A Fetterbrush Christmas

Remembering when I moved to the Blue Ridge Mountains and fishing brings back a lot of old memories – both good and not so good. Sometime back before I (or Almighty God) changed the path of my life, I was married with a wife and bunch of little Fetterbrushes. I remember the holidays at the Fetterbrush house. We had a good Thanksgiving. All the little Fetterbrushes were fat and happy for another few days. They were all looking forward to Christmas and I love this time of the year, too. I remember last year's Christmas day very well. It didn't go as perfect as I had hoped it would. I suppose you might like to hear about it.

Buying presents was a bit tough last year. I had saved $75.00 in my Christmas club savings account. With four children and a stay-at-home wife who all expect much from nothing, I would need to spend $10.00 each on the dear children, leaving $35.00 for the little wife. I went shopping the weekend after Thanksgiving when they put everything on sale. I thought it would be good to take the wife and kids to her mom's so I could shop in peace without them little Fetterbrushes knowing what they would get for

Christmas. I went to the big city of Winston-Salem, North Carolina where I would have plenty of options so I could find the perfect gifts for my beloved family. I arrived in the parking lot of the mall. It took me three hours to get parked. Traffic was a mess. When I finally got parked, I was at the outer edge of the parking lot. I started walking. When I got into the mall, it was a packed madhouse. I worked my way to one of the large department stores. I began in the clothing section. Let's see, Jill was wanting a husband for Christmas (or a baby if a husband couldn't be had), Sally was wanting a car, Johnny was wanting a motorcycle, and Billy was wanting a hunting rifle. The little wife had not suggested anything to me about what she wanted for Christmas.

A store clerk came up to me and asked if she could help me. "Sure," I exclaimed. "What do you have for under ten dollars? I need four presents for my four children; two boys & two girls, ages about 13, 14, 15, and 16, I think, and I plan on spending, with tax, ten dollars each on them. Oh, and there's the little wife. I plan on spending $35.00 on her." The clerk gave me a funny look and suggested I take a look at their catalog for some ideas and walked away. Hmm… must have been on commission or something. I somehow ended up in the women's underwear section. I thought this might be a good place to buy the little missus something. I really hated being in this section, but a real nice middle-aged lady came up and offered to help. She was apparently in charge of the entire women's clothing section of this department store. I explained my desires to her, and she told me that they had some very nice dresses on sale for $29.95. She asked me what size dress my wife wore. I told her that when I hugged the little woman, face to face and chest to chest, I could reach around her tightly and my hands were about two foot apart. I thought that if she could hold up the dress and maybe we could stick some pillows in it to fill it out and I could reach around it to see if it would fit her. She turned away from me really quick. I thought she was choking or something but then she turned around mumbling something about there being no dress in this store that big and suggested I go over to the perfume section. As soon as I walked away, I heard someone bust out laughing over in that women's section. Wished I had got in on that one.

Perfume was a great idea. I would get each of the boys a bottle of some cheap he-man super-smelling after shave lotion that was sure to draw in the girls, and I would get each of the girls a bottle of teen-miss cologne. For the little wife, they had something special imported from the Far East called *Ravishing Tiger* cologne. On its label it stated that "it would make any man your servant". She deserved a helper around the house. The nice girl rang me up. It all came to $73.65 with tax. I pulled out my wallet, and you know, it's a funny thing, that with all the excitement about Christmas shopping, I forgot to get my money out of the bank. The girl started trying to get me to apply for their credit card, but that was no good at all... tried for one of those years ago; didn't work. I asked her if she knew how to get to the closest branch of the bank that I had my Christmas club account with. She said she had never heard of that bank. She brought out a phone book and I called them for directions. They were on the other side of town. They told me they would be open until 5 pm that day. I began the journey back to my car. I knew the general direction, but I forgot to look at the exact line number I was parked in. After some searching, I found my faithful old rusty yellow AMC Pacer.

I started the long journey across the city to find a branch of my bank. It took me about an hour to get onto the main road that would take me across town. I finally arrived at the bank ten minutes before closing. I went in and asked to withdraw my money. It was $75.63 with interest. I told the woman about how I forgot to get my money out. She told me that there was a branch just two blocks from the mall. Oh, well! I was low on fuel, so I started on my trip home.

I thought I would stop in at one of the large, big-box discount stores. Once inside, I was hit by three shopping carts, followed by two gangs looking to rob me, kicked by a brat, shoved into a counter, and something wet was flung on me by a passing baby in one of those car buggy carts. Its mom grinned! I left before anger and frustration messed up my unique shopping experience. I decided that I would *shop at home for the holidays!*

On my way back up the mountain, it occurred to me that everything I needed for Christmas was right there in my small town in the Blue Ridge, with no crowds. I thought about what the kids wanted for Christmas. Jill was wanting a husband (or baby) for Christmas. There were plenty of churches, preachers, photographers, and florists, but I didn't see her finding a man by Christmas that would marry her. Besides, she was too young to marry by at least a year or two. Sally was wanting a car. There were plenty of car dealers. Johnny was wanting a motorcycle. There were many motorcycles for sale in the winter and many dealers in the mountains. Billy was wanting a hunting rifle. There are many good sporting goods stores in the mountains. For the little wife, there were clothing stores, jewelry stores, just about anything I could imagine that my little woman would want. So that's that! I was shopping at home for Christmas.

The next day, I went shopping locally and found the perfect gifts for my perfect loving family for Christmas.

The first week of December, I loaded up the family in the Pacer and drove to one of our favorite local choose & cut Christmas tree farms. We made a day of it. It was really fun. Our favorite farm offered cider and games; had gifts, drawings, and Santa and his sleigh. We picked a nice tree. The kids and my sweetie chipped in and bought the tree. They did not think my choices in the past were good enough. I don't see why they need a 12-foot tree, but they're paying for it. Once the huge tree was tied to the top of the Pacer, we went home, and everyone decorated the tree while I hung some lights around the house. I had to replace a few bulbs, but it all worked out well. It started lightly snowing that evening. It was a perfect day.

On Christmas morning, everyone awoke to find presents under the tree. As they began to open them, I could just see the joy coming from their faces. Jill got a pink wedding planner for keeping up with her wedding plans and a baby naming book. Sally got a cool steering wheel cover and key chain set for her car whenever she could afford one. Johnny got a pair of goggles for his future motorcycle. Billy got a gun-cleaning kit for his hoped-for hunting rifle, and best of all, my sweetie got a $35.00 gift certificate good for one 30-minute therapeutic Swedish massage. Merry Christmas and Happy New Year! "What did I get?" I got the flu from that little sweet lady at the mall! Oh well, might as well laugh about it!

Episode Six: Old Red

When I was about 6 or 7 years old, Daddybrush, (that's what Momma called him) came home with a strange-lookin' creature ridin' in the back of his old Dodge truck. Sure enough, it was a full-grown red and white spotted cow. Daddy was mostly a sharecropper back in those days. We lived on many farms movin' around the south wherever work was available. We had been in this spot for several months. Best I remember, it was an old farm. The owner had built an entire new house, barns and everything just a mile down the road. So, I guess we had a barn. All my brothers and sisters, at least the ones that were old enough to walk, came runnin' out to see that cow. Mommabrush (Daddy's pet name for Momma) come runnin' out, too. I don't think she liked that cow too much. Old Red was a friendly sorta cow. She had a harness and Daddy backed the truck up to a bank and just led her right off the pickup truck. Daddy led Old Red right up to where we were all standin'. Us kids started pettin' on her. Momma said somethin' along the lines of, "What in the world have you done?" About that time Old Red slowly raised her long tail and, well, you know what cows do, especially ones that have been ridin' in the back of a truck for several miles. She did it, too... splattered all over us kids and

Momma. Momma got real spewed up over that. She walked off mumblin' somethin' 'bout how the laws ought to be changed and screamed "you kids get in here and get cleaned up for supper." Daddy walked his new cow into the old barn.

We heard Daddy holler, "Goin' to the store to get some feed." He left. Momma told us kids to stay away from that stupid cow. We had chickens and hogs; I didn't see what havin' a milk cow would hurt. Momma was just gettin' supper on the table when Daddy come walkin' in. It got really quiet in that house. Momma said, "If y'all want anything to eat, better wash up and sit down." Everyone gathered around the table. Momma asked little Johnny to return thanks. Little Johnny started, "Dear Lord, thank you for this food we are about to receive. Lord, please bless Daddy and Momma and all my brothers and sisters. Please bless our house and our crops. And Lord, please have mercy on that stupid cow that Momma's gonna kill before sunup. Amen."

That was an interestin' supper. I thought it might be sort of a last supper. After supper, Daddy went outside. Some of us kids followed. Daddy had found an old peck bucket and a milk stool in the barn. He also found a steel milk strainer and some old strainer pads. This was used to pour the milk through to filter the milk into half-gallon jars. He sent that and the bucket to Momma to wash. I'm glad he didn't send me. He tied Old Red up and poured her some feed. The rest of us finished our chores, feeding the hogs and chickens and checking for eggs. We all gathered 'round as Daddy pondered Old Red's teats. I don't think… no, I know for sure, Daddy had never hand-milked a cow. He had run a milkin' machine a time or two, but he just didn't have the experience to hand-milk Old Red. In a little bit, Momma come walkin' into the barn with a nice shiny bucket (it wasn't the one Daddy sent in) and a bucket of soapy water and a wash rag. "Have ya washed her bag yet?" exclaimed Momma. "Ain't drinkin' no milk from a nasty bag or a rusty bucket!" "Get outta my way," demanded Momma.

She sat down on the wobbly stool and proceeded to wash that cow's bag and teats. When done, she pulled up that bucket and started milkin' that cow like a wild woman. Lord, have mercy! Momma knew how to milk a cow. The evenin' was saved! I think Daddy must have known that, too. In just a few minutes, Momma had that bucket half full of milk. Cats started comin' 'round, and every time one would get too close to Momma, she would squirt it with a shot of milk from Old Red. Them old cats started lickin' the milk off, and before long, every cat in the area was hangin' 'round hopin' to get a fresh squirt of milk from Old

Red. Momma filtered her milk through some muslin draped over some half-gallon mason jars. The next mornin' we had some good rich milk for breakfast. Before long, we were eatin' fresh homemade butter, homemade cottage cheese, homemade whipped cream and strawberries, and my least favorite, buttermilk. Momma could do just about anything with Old Red's rich milk. She loved to drink it and cook with it. I think she liked that old cow better than she let on.

It wasn't long that me and some of my brothers and sisters got the bright idea that we could milk Old Red just like Momma. It was bound to be tried by us kids, sooner or later, come Hades or high water. We truly were on a direct path to Hades. It started out with my sister, Jill, tellin' me that she could milk that cow just like Momma — squirt the cats and everything. I wasn't about to let that challenge go unanswered. We snuck into that old barn one day 'bout noon. Old Red had just walked in from the field. We figured that since she was milked every mornin' and evenin', she ought to have a little milk ready by noon. We walked up and started pettin' her and she seemed to like that.

I pulled up the stool and told Jill to try her out, and it occurred to me that Jill had been tellin' me a fib. Jill wasn't about to touch that cow's teats. No way! Well, I was here, so I might as well learn how to milk a cow. I sat down, talkin' calmly to Old Red. She looked around at me with them big eyes as if to ask, "What do you think you're doin'?" It occurred to me that Daddy always give her some feed to eat. So, I had Jill pour her a cup of cow feed. She began to eat. I started tryin' to figure out this whole milkin' process and I finally got it to work. I squirted a little milk onto the ground. About that time, Old Red swung her tail 'round and hit me right in the face. I fell back. Jill screamed and Old Red made a dash for the door… liked to run me over. That old cow was really scared of Jill's scream. We run to the door and Old Red had busted through the fence and was headin' down the road. Oh, Lord, we were done for! We had done run off Daddy's prize milk cow.

We started runnin' toward the road and Momma hollered, "Lunch is ready." We froze! She hollered again, "Where you kids going in such a hurry?" Answerin' that question would've been a death sentence, at least we thought it would. We worried ourselves sick the rest of the afternoon. Jill kept comin' to me askin', "What are we gonna do?" "We're gonna have to tell!" I knew she was right, but I just couldn't bring myself to tellin' Momma that we had run off the cow.

Daddy came in just in time for supper. Jill and I had been hidin' out and keepin' quiet. We knew time was about to end for us. Durin' supper, Daddy asked, "Max, what are you bein' so quiet for?" I mumbled somethin' 'bout not feelin' good. Jill saved the day by askin' Daddy how his day was. He said, "Funniest thing happened! We're gonna have to build up them old fences. I come in and Old Red was standin' just outside the fence at the driveway gate. I opened the gate and she walked back into the field. Strangest thing! Did you kids see anything?" We were saved! No whippin', no missin' meals. No "stay away from that cow" speeches. The good Lord was truly lookin' out for me and Jill that day. Never again would I try and milk that old cow. Yes sir, buddies. I've learned my lesson. At that moment, little Johnny blurted out, "Yeah, Max and Jill thought they were gonna milk that stupid cow at noon. She looked plumb mad tearin' through that fence. They run her plumb off the farm!" *The End!*

Episode Seven: No Boyfriend for Katie-Lee

One spring, my eldest daughter Katie-Lee was looking for a boyfriend. I'm not her real daddy but that's another story. It was quite possible she was about to go boy crazy. Any boy stupid enough to give my daughter a live pig is a dangerous boy for sure. I remember thinking to myself about all my many messed up tries at marriage and it occurred to me that I had to keep her from dating for as long as I could, especially this slick booger. Back in them days, giving a young girl a pig was just short of a shotgun wedding, so I had to come up with a powerful reason to turn her or the boy she was pondering against dating, at least until she finishes elementary school. I needed a plan.

There was no amount of talking or threatening I could have done to prevent her from talking to or seeing boys. I might have done some good seeking out any boys who show an interest in my daughter, especially with pig gifts, and gently encourage them to remain unattached, at least to my daughter; however, I know this would have been time consuming and potentially dangerous. No, I need a better way — an attack plan. As I remember it, it went something like this back then:

First, I must secure a spy — someone who can keep track of my daughter and report directly to me — someone who will work cheap. Katie-Lee's younger half-sister Gabby was the one for the job. Gabby will spy on, and sell-out just about anyone for the right price and I happen to know she needs money right now. She made a good income when me and her mother were breaking up. It will cost two payments with Gabby; one to acquire her services and another to keep her quiet about it. After a brief discussion and the release of $50 out of the kids Christmas fund, Gabby was on the "Fetterbrush Anti-Dating Plan" payroll. She was to secure and report any pertinent information about Katie-Lee's man-seeking. The information return was almost instant. Within ten minutes after handing her $50, I had learned more things about my first-born daughter than I cared to really know.

With the first step complete, I had to figure out a way to make Katie-Lee less desirable to boys in general. I know girls like to use fancy perfumes and makeup and stuff to draw in the boys. I have heard about special scents designed to draw in the opposite sex. I wonder if there are scents that might repel the opposite sex. Hmm . . . boy repellent. This will require some research and testing. What stinks and would be safe and legal to use? I know trout does not smell so bad when you're eating it, but it is very noticeable to anyone walking into a house where fish have been fried. Boiled eggs are very much the same way. You do not notice them until you leave and come back into the house. Could I come up with an anti-love potion with fish & eggs? I wish Grandma Fetterbrush were still alive. She knew how to make all kinds of potions and cast spells.

Gabby had told me that she had learned that a boy was to take Katie-Lee out for lunch on Monday at school. The plan must be put into operation now. To begin with, I had to cook up some fish & eggs, eat most of them, and save a few pieces back for experimentation. With Gabby's help, I also squeezed some oil out of the fish into a small bottle. Gabby's job was to rub some of this oil onto Katie-Lee before she left for school Monday. The house reeked with fish and egg smell so bad, Katie-Lee didn't notice the extra smell. We strategically placed or rubbed small bits of fish and eggs onto Katie-Lee's clothing that we thought she might wear Monday. Gabby got Katie-Lee to try her new "secret love oil" that would drive the boys crazy. Katie-Lee headed off to school smelling like fish & eggs, only now the fish & eggs had some age on them. The oil was working overtime, too.

It was all I could do to keep Mrs. Fetterbrush from making Katie-Lee stay home and take a bath. I had let her in on our plan, and she was madder than a hornet about the whole thing. There was no boy who would touch Katie-Lee now.

The day went by, and evening arrived. We were all sitting down at the dinner table and Katie-Lee walked in. She reeked awful bad, and we all noticed. Little Johnny said, "Something stinks really bad and it's coming from Katie-Lee. Her new boyfriend must have rubbed off on her." With that statement, Katie-Lee exclaimed, "I met the most wonderful boy today. I think I'm in love. Can I bring him home with me tomorrow to meet you all?" The questions started flowing over the table. "What's his name?" "Tommy." "Where's he from?" "A little town on the coast of Maine." "Do you have a picture?" "Wow, he's cute!" exclaimed Gabby. "What does his parents do for a living?" asked Mrs. Fetterbrush. Katie-Lee stated, "They owned and ran a fishing boat on the coast of Maine until two years ago. Now they run a big chicken farm down off the mountain. It was love at first sight. And by the way Gabby, that magic stuff really works! Oh, them girls that have been picking on me didn't come close today, either. It's been a really cool day."

Well, that's the end of my anti-matchmaking career. I was getting ready for work Tuesday morning, and I happened to notice Gabby in front of her mirror with the little bottle. She was rubbing three-day old fish oil all over her neck. She smelt like a fish factory as she walked by. I stated with a grin, "Have a nice day at high school honey!" Life is a strange thing.

Episode Eight: Max's Credit Card

One day Max stepped out to the mailbox, and inside it was this nice fancy envelope that stated, "Open immediately" - "0% Interest, No Yearly Fee"! Max enthusiastically opened the flap and inside was this fancy plastic card with a picture of a sunny beach on the front along with some numbers and by gosh, his name was on it, too. He had heard about these once or twice but had never experienced the pleasure of owning one before.

Well, Max wasn't one to read "between the lines", so he read the bold advertising, (paid no mind to the small print), tossed the rest into the home-dug trash dump back of the house, and stuck the card into the chest pocket of his overalls. Now, Max wasn't a dumb feller; he just hadn't any knowledge about how credit cards worked. As far as bartering and so forth, he was the best in the valley.

That evening while sitting at the supper table with his beloved Fanny, (the current Mrs. Fetterbrush), Max pulled out the credit card. Why, Fanny's eyes got bigger than moon pies! "Max!" she exclaimed. "How did you get hold of one of them cards?" Max answered, nonchalantly, "Sent to me US

Mail, darlin'; guess that company knew I needed something for <u>Free</u>." Well, Fanny's side of the family didn't fall too far from the old tree. She said, "Well, what are we waitin' for? Let's go somewhere and try it out." "Okay," answered Max. "Tie yourself on back of the moped, and let's ride!"

First stop was the country store and gas-up station. Max filled up the moped while Fanny loaded up on snacks inside. Max went in and the storekeeper said, "That'll be $17.44 total. Cash or card?" Hmm, "Card," answered Max, as he handed it to the storekeeper with a big grin on his face. Oh, he felt bigger than a 'Rockefeller'. "Sign here," said the man. Max made his mark and handed the paper back to him. In turn the storekeeper handed Max a copy. "Oh, thank you," said Max, and he put the paper in his side pocket.

They climbed back aboard the moped and were off. Fanny hollered to Max, "See how easy that was! My, my...all you have to do is go in, get whatever you want, make your mark on a little piece of paper, and it's <u>Free!</u> No money, no trade! Ain't that somethin' Max, honey?" "It sure enough is!" Max hollered back to Fanny.

As they puttered on down the backroad alongside the Interstate, Max decided to continue on to the big city. He thought they might as well put that card to good use, since that company said it was <u>Free</u>. They pulled up to the fanciest hotel he ever saw. Boy, it was a sight. Fancy cars were parked all around it and people were going inside in a hurry. "Come on, Fanny. We better get in there quick before all the rooms get filled up," said Max. Max took off running as Fanny bounced along a few feet behind. Once inside, they got behind a line of people. When it was their turn, a lady at the desk asked if she could help them. "We'd like the best room you got!" proclaimed Max. "Yeah, with a fancy tub," said Fanny. "I'm a bit dusty from the ride." The lady at the desk gave them the once over up and down. "Are you sure you can afford it? Uh, we do serve upper clientele you know!" Max pulled out the card and handed it to the lady. "Do you have identification, sir?" "Of course, I do." answered Max. "I'm not dumb, you know!" Max reached into his back pocket and pulled out his well-worn birth certificate. "Carry it with me all the time in case of these very situations," said Max.

The lady said she'd have to check it out... so, after a few minutes, she came back and said, "Well, you are who you say you are, and the card company verified you. Room 777 is available, the best in the house. I need to swipe your card, sir." "Hey, you're not swipin' my card from me-I just got it today in the mail! You get your own card," Max yelled. "You don't understand, sir," said the lady. "I just meant I need to insert your card in this little machine so it can read your information for me." "Well, what about that, Fanny. That little machine's gonna read my card to the lady. I'm sorry, ma'am. I didn't know you had a "literate" problem. Excuse me! Wow, what'll they think of next, Fanny…a machine that reads to people." The lady at the desk was so dumbfounded she wasn't even going to justify with an answer. She just handed back the card and the paper for Max to make his mark, gave him his copy and continued about her business.

A feller in a red jacket came along and asked Max if he had anything to be carried up. "Nope, we travelled light, tonight," said Max. Show us the way, though. The feller showed them to a door. It opened up and several people got out of a tiny room. "Going up?" asked another feller who Max noticed was pushin' buttons on the inside of the door. "Take them up to the seventh floor, please," said the first feller. Max and Fanny stepped inside. The door closed. Max and Fanny were aghast! "Hey, if this is our room, young feller, I'd be obliged if you'd leave…we don't really need a "third party" if you get my drift!" exclaimed Max. "Oh, no sir," answered the young feller. "This is the elevator. It takes you up to where your room is!" The feller punched button #7, the elevator began to move, and Max and Fanny thought it was as fun as the chute and ladder ride at the firehouse fair back home.

The elevator door opened, and the feller directed them to their room. He showed them how to open their door with a key card. They stepped inside. "Wow!" said Fanny. "It's like a mansion!" The feller held out his hand in anticipation. Max finally figured out that he was waitin' for a tip. "Oh, yeah, tell 'em down at the desk to put it on my card. It's free, you know; give to me by a nice company." Max said with utmost pride. Max and Fanny roamed around the room and soon became acquainted with all the niceties that came with being in a swanky hotel.

After about a week of fun and frolicking, winin' & dinin', a knock came at the door. The hotel manager was there inquiring if they were enjoying their stay. "Oh, we're havin' a dandy time, somethin' we couldn't have done if not for that company sendin' me that card for <u>Free</u> stuff," answered Max. "Well, that's why I'm here, sir," said the manager. "Unfortunately, you have reached your limit on your card and I'm afraid you'll have to give up your room, now." "Oh, well, alright! I guess we don't wanna wear out our welcome. Come on Fanny...time to go home. Thank you, my good man, for all the <u>Free</u> food and amenities. Maybe that company will send us another complimentary card sometime and we'll see you again!" Max declared.

Max and Fanny puttered back home on the moped delighting in their spur-of-the-moment vacation. As they arrived, they first pulled up to the mailbox. Inside were two fancy envelopes. They drove up to the house, opened them up, and behold, more cards offering 0% Free...uh, that's all it took, just one look at that one little word. No reading the fine print! "Gosh," said Max. "C'mon Fanny! Seems like we're going on another vacation."

By now you understand that they had never experienced ownership of a credit card before and were not up on reading the legalities. All they saw in big bold letters was 0% Interest FREE, NO yearly fee! FREE being the key word, here. Again, these was one of those cards that activates the first time you use it and it was from a different bank than the first one.

After extra feed was left out for the animals, they ran into the house, grabbed some clean garb, went out and hopped onto the moped, and off they sped! Back at the same old store and gas-up station, they filled up and gathered some munchies. The storekeeper asked, "Cash or Card?" "Card!" yelled Max, with uppity pride. "Hey, before you add up the total, would you happen to have one of them there hool-ee dancin' dolls? You know; the ones with the grass skirts that bobbles back and forth whilst sittin' on the handlebars of my ride? It'll give me somethin' to help me stay awake durin' the trip." Max leaned closer to the storekeeper and whispered, "Keeps the Missus guessin', too, if you know what I mean?"

The storekeeper reached under the counter and handed Max a box with the doll inside. He totaled up everything and handed Max the paper saying, "You need to sign it, sir," and gave Max the copy. Max and Fanny hurried out. Max opened up the box and there was the prettiest little hool-ee doll wearing a grass skirt and flowers were hanging around her neck (and to Max's amazement not much of anything else!) Max attached her to the bars of the moped, gave it a bit of a jiggle, hopped up front of Fanny and they were off to a new destination.

Up the hills and down the valleys they rode. When Max got a bit tired, he just eyeballed his little hool-ee girl and it gave him the push he needed to keep on going. Max thought, "Huh! Maybe one of these days if I accidentally run this moped across a big hole and Fanny happens to bounce off and get lost, and I decide to trade up, then. . . ." About that time, he hit a small hole and Fanny squeezed up on him for dear life. "Oh, well. Better safe than sorry, I guess, (or better luck next time)!" thought Max devilishly.

After traveling all night long and into the wee hours of the morning, they came upon this huge mansion out in the middle of nowhere. It was still kind'a dark, but the lights surrounding the place made it look almost like Christmas to Max and Fanny. "I've seen pictures of these places on the walls whilst visitin' the local, uh, I mean whilst visitin', said Max. Fanny gave Max a look that let him know she just wasn't an everyday dumb blonde and she knew what he meant. Many a night she pretended to be asleep when he came trippin' in lookin' for a spot to hide his jug.

Anyway, Max held onto the moped so Fanny could pry herself off the seat. Being as it wasn't quite daybreak, there was no parking attendant; so, Max just rolled the moped over beside some bushes and a big stone fountain, making sure it wouldn't be in the way of other travel. They walked up these big stone steps and into the doors of the big mansion. A big chandelier lit up the inside and a red carpet led to a desk. They walked to the desk and no one was in sight, so they rang a bell that was on the counter. Eventually, a sleepy-eyed well-dressed feller appeared. "Sorry for inconveniencin' you at this time of the mornin', but we're tired, too. Could we have a room?" asked Max. Well, the feller wasn't quite up to speed being it was so early, so he rushed through and gave Max and

Fanny a room on the top floor and directed them to the elevator. "Uh… don't you need my card?" asked Max. "Oh, yeah!" answered the feller, and he grabbed the card and quickly swiped it in the machine. A paper printed out and he hurried Max to make his mark, no questions asked and sent them on their way.

Up, up, up in the elevator they went 'til they reached the top. They found the room as per the directions the feller gave them. When they stepped inside, they were more excited than seeing the last place they stayed at. As you well know, Max and Fanny took every advantage because as Max put it, "It's FREE, you know." Just like the time before, a knock at the door occurred and another well-dressed feller explained to Max and Fanny that they were at their limit. Max shook his head and said, "Yes sir, we understand it's time to go, but maybe we'll get another one of them FREE cards so we can come back again sometime." The feller was quite confused but didn't comment except for, "Maybe so, sir."

Max and Fanny took off once more for home. (Max was still ponderin' that big hole, but every time he ran over one, Fanny squeezed onto him tighter than crossin' the one before). Finally, they arrived back at their place and first thing's first, they opened up the mailbox. There was only one envelope inside addressed to "Mr. Maximillian Fetterbrush" and stamped in big bold red letters: OPEN IMMEDIATELY. Max recognized the envelope as being from the same card company as the first two with the words "FREE" and "NO YEARLY FEE" on them, but this one was a bit different. Under "Open Immediately" it was stamped "PAYMENT DUE IN 30 DAYS". Max and Fanny pondered over it for a minute and decided there must have been some mistake. After all, to Max, "FREE" meant "<u>FREE</u>"! They drove on up to the door; Max heaved Fanny gently off the moped, as he gave a little wink towards the hool-ee doll as to say, "Keep watchin'."

Once inside the house, Fanny opened the envelope, and lo and behold she dropped to the floor with a bounce. Max ran over to her yellin', "Fanny, Fanny, are you alright?" She was out cold. Max ran outside to the well and pumped some water, ran back to Fanny and doused her good. As she came to, she sat up and had the most dumbfounded look of surprise on her face. "Fanny, what in tarnation caused you to keel over like that?" asked Max. Fanny couldn't find the words, but she clumsily handed the piece of mail to Max. Max wasn't much of a reader as you well know, but he recognized enough to "put two and two together". The paper said "Total Charges $7777.77, First Payment due in 30 days. "Whew! Seems like this here company is a bit on the crooked side, don't you think so, Fanny?" he nonchalantly asked her. "First, they give you the bait, then they won't let you keep the fish, so to speak! Well, FREE means FREE, and by gosh, we'll just ignore it and things'll work out okay, Fanny." Fanny came to her senses but wasn't sure why Max was takin' it all in stride.

After 30 days, nothing happened. Then a week or so later, another piece of mail arrived. This one was stamped PAST DUE, PAY IN FULL. As before, Max ignored it. Another 30 days went by, nothin'. After 90 whole days, a big black Cadillac pulled up to their place and a man in a fancy suit got out totin' a fancy piece of luggage. Max met him at the door; "Afternoon," said Max. "Good day to you. My name is Mr. Needleum from the Needleum Legal Associates. Our motto is "For collection, let us Needle 'Um for you!" He continued on about why he was there, and unfortunately, it wasn't to give Max and Fanny any FREE advice.

Well, after a lengthy conversation, and Mr. Needleum explainin' that nothin' was ever FREE, Max and Fanny didn't give up the thought that FREE meant FREE. Max said, "If it was sent to me FREE and it says FREE, then why ain't it FREE?" Mr. Needleum went on to explain, "Well, sir, CREDIT means CREDIT, and that's why it's called a CREDIT CARD. You CHARGE what you want and pay later."

Max thought for a minute or two and replied, "Don't know nothin' 'bout credit, just know FREE means FREE." Well, again, Mr. Needleum tried very hard to make them understand, but to no avail. He said, "Don't you understand that I'm here to collect a debt, and if you can't pay up, well, I guess we'll have to seek restitution by other means." Max thought this was a bunch of hogwash but was very cool about the whole situation for some reason. "FREE means FREE, and nobody can tell me any different!" He chased Mr. Needleum away with a pitchfork. Mr. Needleum yelled, "I'll be back with help next time."

The next day, the big black Cadillac came driving up with a police car behind it. Mr. Needleum got out of the Cadillac, and some feller with a badge got out of the other car. "Apparently, he's some kind of lawman," thought Max. Over and over again, Max got the same explanation as before. "Seems like we're getting nowhere," said Mr. Needleum to the Official. "How in the world do we proceed?" The Official just shook his head, through his hands up in the air; and he figured if you couldn't make someone understand that FREE doesn't necessarily mean FREE, then how do you explain to Max that debt collectin' can mean takin' anything and everything of any value that he had to suffice payin' what he owed, that Max insisted he didn't owe in the first place, "cause it was FREE!"

Well, to make a long story short, Max got out of any payin' so it really was FREE! A professional criminal psychologist was called in to examine Max. He gave his medical opinion and he proclaimed, "Mr. Fetterbrush is on the brink of insanity or is a total genius. Forcing the issue and making him pay for something that he claims to not understand could either send him over the edge or make him the wealthiest mobster alive." Fanny, naturally, was off the hook, anyways, cause her name wasn't even on the card and she made no mark on any of the little slips of paper (one thing Max didn't think of). Max's true cash worth was not of value to the credit card company; they didn't barter with pigs and chickens and such and Max's ped wasn't worth much at auction. The moped wouldn't even bring 30% of book value and so they didn't bother trying to take it as any payment. It all came down to the flaky attorney, Mr. Needleum, who knew he would be fighting a losing battle for even thinking he could get rich off of either side, so he only collected his expenses from the credit card company for hiring him for services rendered, and he went back to the city a little less wealthy.

As for Max; shortly thereafter, he received another card in the mail (they just kept on coming). He knew not to press his luck. He hopped on his moped, took a slow, relaxing ride, beaming with pride at such a clever accomplishment. As he watched the little hool-ee girl dancin' on the handlebars, he spoke to her as if she were a livin' person, "Nothin' is ever free in this ol' world hool-ee girl, but it's how to play the game that gives a man pleasure; and, hool-ee girl, there's a live one just like you beyond these hills, and I'll keep my eye out for her… 'til I find a big enough hole!" And, he smiled and gave her a wink.

Episode Nine: Soup Beans

Do you ever reminisce of the good ole days, back when soup beans had real flavor, real salt, real soup, real pork side meat, mmm… and GAS! For about the past three weeks I have been craving some of Mama's, (God rest her soul), good ole soup beans. So, in this article I will tell you about my one attempt, many years ago, to cook Soup Beans, like my Momma did, (God rest her soul).

Tryin' to recollect exactly how momma cooked them was the first problem. I remember when I was a kid, something in the kitchen goin', "chiga, chiga, chiga, chiga, chiga, chiga…" like a Choo-Choo train. My Momma must of had a, I think what was called a pressure cooker. I am sure that before that she used a plain old pot to cook them all in, but I want them quick, so the pressure cooker will have to do. Where would I find a pressure cooker?

I went to the local flea market and looked for a nice sized pressure cooker to cook my soup beans in, assuming there would be a recipe with the box. A sweet little grandma looking woman with a table of kitchen utensils just happened to have what I was looking for. A slightly used pressure cooker, no box, for 30 bucks. She guaranteed it to be almost new. Said it cost her over $100 new. Sweet of her to give me such a fine deal on an almost new pressure cooker. Upon getting' home, I asked my then current wife (not sure which one it was) if she knew how to use a pressure cooker, and after a few certain words of encouragement, she told me you put in whatever it is you plan on cooking, cover it with water, put the lid on, the jiggler, and turn the stove on, and cook it for however long the recipe says. I had bought me a pound of dried soup beans at the flea market. I poured them in the pressure cooker, covered them with water, throwed in a handful of salt, (probably got too much water, but it was within an inch of the top), put the lid on it, and turned the stove to high. After a while, steam started shooting out the hole on top, (kids don't try this at home). So, I figured it was a good time to drop the little jiggler on and it sealed right up. At that point, I seen the little wife taking the kids and mumble something about going to her mom's for the rest of the day. And there was that magical sound, "chiga, chiga, chiga, chiga, chiga, chiga…" and it was getting faster and faster. So, I thought now would be a great time to cut the heat down a little. It sounded pretty good now, just as I remember when I was a kid. Thought I would go try to call up my Aunt Sally-Ann and see if she knew how long I should cook these beans.

She asked me if I had soaked them overnight. I said no, I skipped that step, "Did you look them for rocks and stones?" "Nope," I said "Skipped that too." She said I should cook them about 20 or 30 minutes, or until they're done. Hmmm… 20 or 30 minutes that gives me time to go chop some wood. I could hear that "chiga, chiga, chiga, chiga, chiga, chiga, all the way out in the wood pile. I had busted several sticks of wood when all of a sudden, I heard that chiga, chiga, chiga, chiga, come to an abrupt end. Then I heard a distinct pop or small explosion sound and then a loud spewing sound. I started making tracks to that stove. About halfway up the steps there was a very loud ka-boom. Upon arriving in the kitchen, there was steam spewing and beans dripping from the ceiling. Parts of that cooker were layin' all the way down the hall. Good thing the wife (not sure which one she was) and the kids were gone to Mommy-in-law's (at least I was glad the kids were gone). Anyway, I finally got the stove cut off, and began to start pondering on cleanin' up the mess.

At that time, our trailer had a kind-of open kitchen, living area and one of the bedrooms was open into the kitchen, and not one square inch of any space was left uncovered from beans and bean soup. Boy did it smell good! Momma would be proud (God rest her soul)! I tasted a few of the beans and they didn't seem done enough yet. I raked and scraped and shoveled… wiped, mopped, and finally got most of the beans back into what was left of the cooker. Mostly what blew was the lid and related attachments. I thought if I could just get them beans to cook a little longer without a lid, they might be eatable, then it occurred to me that I might be eating some metal, so I decided to dump the rest outback, so Spot and the other animals could try some half-cooked soup beans.

When I went back in the trailer, the old trailer ceiling had fell in. It was some kind of old paper board that didn't like the extra weight of the scalding steam and water. I hurried and cleaned it up out of the floor; maybe the little woman won't notice the hole in the ceiling. I had just about come to a mild state of depression at this point. Actually, I was real low. I had dreamed about eating Momma's soup beans for three days, skipped breakfast this morning, could almost taste 'em, so close but yet so far away. Oh well, the Fetterbrush motto; "There is nothing that overcomes depression like going to town and spending some money!"

I went to the local grocery store, to see if I could find some other foods to eat up, I was pretty hungry by now. And right there in the middle of aisle number four, slapped me right in the face like a baseball bat, staring at me like an eagle getting ready to pounce its prey, was those magic words… Suddenly, it all come back to me. Momma never used a pressure cooker at all. That chiga, chiga, chiga, chiga must of come from some old TV show with an old steam powered train in it. There they were in red and yellow "LUCK'S® Homestyle Pinto Beans". I remember as a kid, seeing those empty cans sittin' everywhere on bean day! So, about an hour later, I sat by the warmth of my electric plug-in heater, a 12" black and white T.V. and a giant bowl of boiling hot LUCK'S® pintos with onions, (didn't have a clue how to make cornbread, maybe I will try that adventure at a later time)!

About an hour had passed, and two or three cans of LUCK'S® later, little wife shows up, made a big bold fine statement sayin', "Smells real good in here. Did you actually get them soup beans to cook?" I said "Sure honey, there's a whole pot sitting over on the stove." As she meandered towards the stove, I started hearing something that sounded like a basketball coach throwin' down on the referees. She was really throwin' a fit! Unlike anything I had ever seen before… "What is all this #%#@* mess inside my stove?!" It never occurred to me that some of the beans were still inside the stove, under the stove, and had dripped into the oven. I got up tryin' to make a beeline for the door, but as soon as I hit my feet… there it came! An explosion that almost equaled what happened over that stove a few hours ago...Those beans were really workin' (producing much gas) and so was the little wife. I saw a pot come flyin' over the couch! Oh well, I made it to the back door just in time. About time for a new wife anyway!

Episode Ten: Shoveling

I remember the weather forecaster telling us that the chances of snow on Christmas was something like 1000 to 1, partially due to global warming and other factors. That was about three weeks before Christmas. Also, I remember some expert predicting that this winter would be much warmer than previous winters, thanks to global warming. I was so thankful to not have to do last minute Christmas shopping with the newest little lady due to the massive snowfall and extreme cold weather that kicked in somewhere on the weekend before Christmas. I am really thankful for global warming. Finally, a beautiful, cold, snowy winter at home with my wonderful sweetie, the driveway packed with snow, no Christmas presents (couldn't get to the shopping center), and no way Santa was going to show up at my house, just wasn't good enough!

A couple of days after Christmas my little sweetie informed me that we were out of milk, bread, dog food, eggs, ham, potted meat, Vienna's, corn cheese puffs, crackers, vanilla wafers, beans and weenies and most of the other good stuff necessary for survival. She informed me we had $65 in the checkbook, and that the grocery store was open if I would get my sorry butt up and clean out the driveway so we could get our car to town! I was just sitting and enjoying the beautiful 7-degree temperature and hard-packed snow, when all this came upon me. Okay, so I will go shovel snow.

It was frozen so hard that I had to bust it loose with an old tater-hoe and haul the chunks off with my shovel. I finally got a path from the back of my AMC Pacer to the edge of the hard-top road when a road grader came by and filled her back in! Oh, well… uh… a little more digging and we will be ready to go to town. I never go to the grocery store with my sweetie, so this should be an experience! In fact, I haven't been in the grocery store in years.

Upon arriving at the grocery store, I decided to go in and push the buggy and check out any new things being offered. I also had to keep Sweetie from spending too much money. Sweetie reminded me once again that we only had $65 in the checkbook, and I reminded her that I wasn't the one that spent all the money for groceries. As we went down the first aisle, it occurred to me that there were a lot of potential new wives for Max walking around in this place (should the need ever occur). But I couldn't let Sweetie notice that I was eye-balling future potential Fetterbrushes, just in case! I think Sweetie was number five, but I'm not really sure.

This is cool! I didn't realize that they sell videos in the grocery store. And there are those real good name brand corn cheeses I haven't had in 20 years. As we come around the third aisle, there was the latest Rifle and Handgun magazines and the new Used Car Price Guide. Hmm... This is a pretty cool place. My gosh, right there in aisle seven are tools and propane cylinders. Gotta have some propane for the camp stove in case the power goes out. And, would you believe, right there out of the blue, an old friend from high school runs up and hugs me… "Max, is that you?" "Yep!" It was my old girlfriend Layola from Oxford High School in Southern Louisiana. "What are you doing in the Blue Ridge Mountains, Layola?" "Oh, I'm just passing through on my way back home from visiting Aunt Sal up in Bluefield. Thought I'd stop and get some grub to snack on. Good to see you, Max!" After some more hugging and reminiscing, my dear Sweetie got really mad. She kinda throwed a fit right there in aisle eight. A real Sweetie-style fit. "Good to see you Layola. Take care." Back to shopping.

I found steaks for half price, pork & beans - buy one, get one free, and potted meat three for $1.00. This place is awesome! Finally, to the checkout Sweetie and I go. After a few minutes I heard the girl at the register tell Sweetie it would be $188.44. When

Sweetie asked me firmly what to do, I told her I guess she would have to put something back. As another fit erupted, I made tracks for the front door. I noticed Layola loading up in the back of a pick-up truck with a camper shell. I hollered, "Hey Layola, you married?" "Nope!" she replied. "Got any extra room in that truck for an old friend?" "Sure, come on get up front with me," Layola replied. I've been needing a vacation anyway. Be good to see Louisiana again. It ought to be really warm down there, too. Might wet a hook in the Mississippi. During Sweetie's fit, I managed to get one of those large paper sacks of groceries in my hands on the way out of the store. Once we were on our way, we learned it had a pack of those steaks, a can of pork & beans, two cans of potted meat, a bag of corn cheeses, this year's gun buyers guide, and a six pack of cold beer, and a box of extra-extra-extra-large feminine pads. The beer and pads were Sweeties but that's ok! We can use the pads to insulate the camper shell if the weather turns cold and they make good tinder for a campfire. I loved those old large paper shopping bags. The old timers called them pokes. "Layola, you got a propane stove in this truck?" "Yep, there's a small one behind the seat." "Good deal! We'll have steak and beans for supper! You sure are looking mighty good, Layola, since I saw you last." Layola looked really nice with her new false teeth, glowing bright red hair, and drops of summer sweat slowly running down her freckled cheeks, all glistening in the light of evening setting sun. "Layola, you never did tell me why your momma named you Layola!" Life is great!

Episode Eleven: Rabbit Hunting

I saw a commercial on TV the other day about Easter and it occurred to me that I have not been a rabbit huntin' for many a year. Should I use a shotgun or a .22 rifle? Hmm, shotgun gets the job done, but a .22 is more sporting and there is no shot to pick out of my teeth while eating Mr. Rabbit. For all you tender hearts out there, rabbit is food! Ok? Ok! It's a .22 long rifle for Mr. Rabbit. It was the first day of rabbit season and I went out in the brush (mountains) where there has to be many a rabbit (and many a hunter). I took me a few fresh carrots just in case rabbits really liked 'em… you know the cartoons and such. (I had never really been rabbit huntin' before, but I did have a really good recipe for bar-b-q'd rabbit). When I finally got to the back country, I strategically placed a few carrots in a location where I thought them rabbits might frequent. I carefully hid myself in the brush and waited. "Come on home to papa (and his big cookin' pot), Mr. Rabbit." I waited, and waited, and waited. Finally, out from cover came what had to be the biggest rabbit ever created on Earth. That giant rabbit jumped out from nowhere and sniffed and looked, and paused - and came step-by-step, a little closer to one of them carrots, and a little closer to my cookin' pot.

I watched and patiently waited until the best opportunity for the shot, and as I looked at Mr. Rabbit through my 6-power scope, it occurred to me that this was a really beautiful creature. In fact, that was the prettiest rabbit I had ever laid eyes on. It must be a girl rabbit. The more I looked, the more I knew that there was no way I could pierce her heart with a .22 long rifle bullet. In fact, I had decided that a burger would be acceptable for dinner (sorry, cow) and the rabbit must live for another day. All of a sudden, I heard shots from guns around me. They were trying to kill "my" rabbit! It was the first day of rabbit season, but this was "my" rabbit. I had clearly decided that she must live, and they had no right to try and take her away from me. She was mine and that was that!

As their shots rang out, I felt my body tense up into an uncontrollable mass of response. I remember running toward that helpless, defenseless, poor dumb rabbit and jumping wildly over her to protect her from the hunters. I flung my body over this beautiful rabbit and screamed "I will save you, sweetie." The firing from the hunters stopped as I heard what seemed to sound like laughter coming from the brush. I had won! This poor, dumb, helpless, defenseless creature would live for another day, thanks to me.

All of a sudden, that rabbit sunk about two inches of teeth into my chest. It hurt something aw…ful bad! And she wouldn't let go. What are you doing you stupid rabbit? I saved you from the cookin' pot! She dug in a little deeper. I said, "Rabbit, you let go of me or I am going to send you on home to your maker." You know what? That rabbit urinated on me. She just soaked my shirt and pants and sunk her teeth in a little deeper.

Oh, right! This is it! I had a fully loaded .22 rifle and I decided, in deep pain, that it was me or this insane rabbit. I said, "Rabbit, it's you or me, and guess who will win? Don't mess with me you crazy rabbit!" That rabbit sunk her teeth in deeper and it was bleeding like crazy and startin' to smart a bit. I pointed the muzzle of my rifle toward that evil, crazy, insane, gigantic, satanic rabbit from Hades and pulled the trigger and it went right through the foot… my foot! Ms. Rabbit sunk her teeth in a little deeper into my chest and I screamed… and cussed. It was on now!

After a fierce fight and much bleeding and cussin', she dropped to the ground and quickly disappeared into the mountains with not a scratch on her. I fell to the ground in pain. I heard the laughter from hunters all around me. I could hear that evil rabbit and all her family laughing from a distance, too. It sounded like a bunch of high-pitched hee-hees. I wrapped my handkerchief around my poor old foot and hobbled off back to my truck. I duck taped the two big bleeding gashes in my chest. That dang rabbit had nearly taken one of my nipples off. I'll be back — with heavy artillery, and body armor. I hope the ER has forgotten about that little incident that occurred last month. Surely, they will patch me up. No puny rabbit gonna outsmart Max. I wonder what's in rabbit urine. I feel kind of faint. That danged old rabbit. I'll be back, when able! It was a two-hour drive out of the mountain and at least 30 miles to the hospital. As I was starting to get the old truck up to speed on that old mountain trail, that dang girl rabbit jumped right out in front of me and over the bank me and my old truck went. If that cliff hadn't had several large oak trees to stop my descent, old Max would have been kilt.

Episode Twelve: Crazy Rooster

I remember when I was a kid back home on the farm. I miss those days. Ma & Pa are gone, the old workhorse has long since vanished from the seals of envelopes, and the old tractor is sittin' in a heap of rust at the bottom of some creek with other collectibles just a-waitin' for the EPA to come and dig 'em up from their restful sleep. I remember about whippin's with a belt; turpentine and corn cobs; burnt motor oil and mangy dogs; foxes in the henhouse; usin' hand clippers instead of Weed Eaters®; eatin' grapes, red raspberries, and "tommy toes" right off the vine and, "clean your plate boy". I miss those little green apples, cardboard & clothespin motors for our bicycles, and fresh fried tenderloin and scratch biscuits on hog killin' & cannin' day.

Yeah, I know; I'm reminiscin', but sometimes it seems good for us to remember the past. If we forget the past, we may not know how to deal with the future. I remember one time when I was about 5 years old, I had been tauntin' the chickens all 'round the yard with my homemade laurel slingshot. Pa had brought in a new big red rooster one mornin', turned him loose, and Pa left for the fields. I hadn't met that ole rooster yet, but I was bored, and it was just a matter of time before me, and that new old crazy rooster would meet up. As I meandered around the farm with my slingshot and a few small pea gravels (borrowed from the newly tarred and pea graveled road in front of the house), I found various targets - a tree, the side of the house, an old bottle in the burnin' pile, and the side of the shed that, unbeknownst to me, rested that big old red rooster. Apparently, I had 'wakened him from a restful sleep, and he was mad. As I reloaded my slingshot, that ole rooster came runnin' 'round the side of that shed, mad, wings raised, and in full flogging mode. He crawled all over my head before I could even think of getting' off a shot. Sure did cut and bleed me good before he ran off. I remember runnin' and screamin' into the house; bleedin', I told Ma about that mean ole rooster. No sooner than I could get the words out of my mouth, Ma yanked me up exclaiming, "You been shootin' at them chickens!" Before I could say anything, Ma washed me off, patched me up, gave me a standard whippin' with a switch, and took my slingshot away. Ma told me to go to bed, and she left the house.

In the meantime, that ole rooster went into the henhouse to brag and glorify his "takin' out the local kid". As I laid there weepin' and thinkin' about that evil rooster, I heard an uprisin' in the chicken coop. It sounded like a fox had gotten in the henhouse. Then all was quiet. I was afraid to get up and wondered if that ole rooster had gotten Ma, too. A few minutes passed by, and Ma came in with a bloody head carryin' that rooster by the feet. Yep, it had flogged her, too. She had done wrung the neck of that old Satanic bird, chopped his head off on the choppin' block and decided to have chicken and dumplin's for supper.

She walked by my room and said, "Wanna help me pluck this bird?" "Sure," I replied. Revenge is sweet! I helped her pluck and clean that old rooster and helped her make dumplin's for supper. She told me several times that it would be best not to mention any of this to Pa when he got in. That ole rooster had really cut her head good. She washed up while the chicken and dumplin's were cookin'. About that time Pa got home.

"Sump'n sure smells good; must be havin' chicken and dumplin's for supper!" Pa exclaimed. The rest of my brothers and sisters had gotten in from school (I must have been too young for school yet) and started commentin' about them good smellin' chicken and dumplin's. Ma made the best chicken and dumplin's anywhere. In about an hour, supper was ready. Ma called everybody to the table.

Eatin' at our house was a real event. The table was covered with food. A big pot of chicken and dumplin's, mashed taters, pickled beans and corn, peas, blackberry sonker, leftover biscuits, and other leftovers from previous days. There was never really enough room for plates and glasses. We were really blessed. About all of this food came off the farm. By the time everybody sat down, plates were already being filled up with food. There was no grace or other formal startin' procedures other than just sittin' down and diggin' in. If you put sump'n on your plate, you were expected to eat it even if you didn't like it. There were many people much poorer than us who would love to have what we have, so Ma would tell us.

The chicken and dumplin's and all the other foods were great as usual. Pa started the supper talk by tellin' us what a rough day he had and statin', "By the way, I picked up a new rooster from up at the stock sale early yesterday morning. He ought to help get them hens back to layin' eggs." "I wouldn't count on it," Ma replied in a low tone with a little grin. Pa asked her what she said, and she just told him to never mind. She looked at me and smiled.

Episode Thirteen: Married Again

I think I just survived another 4th of July celebration. Somehow, I got married again; well, I think I'm married. It was a really rough week all said and done. Her name is Pootsie Fetterbrush. I think she's number 7 or 8. Not quite sure. Doesn't really matter. My last wife just up and left town in the middle of June. Two weeks without a wife was all I could take. I took a wife huntin' trip down toward the Mississippi River Valley, and right there at sunrise, at the Twin Bridges Trailer Park, Motel and Game Room stood the next Mrs. Fetterbrush. She was standin' next to the washin' machine room with a basket of clothes. The sun was glistening off the bead of sweat on her brow, and as she turned, she smiled at me. She was a short, healthy gal, 'bout 4-feet tall with mixed gray, black, and red hair; prettiest thing my eyes have set on in a while, least two weeks. "You married?" I asked. "Nope! That sorry bum left me and all them screamin' kids nearly two weeks ago. Run off with some woman up in the mountains of North Carolina." "Hmm… Could it be he ran off with my… no, couldn't be." "Me too," I told her. "Wanna get married?" I asked. "Will there be a honeymoon?" she asked. "Sure," I said. "How does Gatlinburg Tennessee sound? We can go up and get a nice room and get hitched at one of those weddin' chapels." She said, "Let's Go!" I asked her 'bout the kids and she said, "They'll be fine - let's go." I loaded her up in the Pacer and off we went toward Tennessee. She told me her name was Pootsie. What a name! I made her a poem with her name in it and everything. It was true love at first sight!

We pulled into a junkyard somewhere near the Tennessee state line to get a new front tire for the Pacer. The threads were showin' and I was havin' to add air at about every gas station. It's amazin' how much junkyard tires cost now. I found a good one for $8.00 but they charged $10.00 to put it on for me. Oh well, that's just $18.00 less for the honeymoon suite. We finally got to Gatlinburg… had to sleep in the Pacer for two nights. Pootsie is not real fond of my AMC Pacer. She's a tad overweight and her belly rubbed against the dash and gave her a bit of a rash. I guess that's why they call 'em compact cars. She sure gets good gas mileage - the Pacer, I mean. I had no idea how high honeymoon suites in these motels are. It was the week of the 4th of July. Most of the motels were booked up. We finally found one that had a weddin' suite, but they wanted almost $500 a night. Wow! "What can I get for $25.00," I asked. That man at the desk got all heated up… threatened to call the law on me and everything. "Pootsie honey, let's get married and then worry 'bout where to stay." We went from chapel to chapel. They all wanted birth certificates and ID's. I didn't even have a driver's license and I'm sure Pootsie didn't either. We finally found a woman who said she knew a preacher who would marry us for $20, no questions asked. Now that's right up my alley.

We found him in a small shack 'bout five miles up in the mountain. He had been celebrating the night before. We finally got him on his feet, and he married us, filled out the marriage certificate, and a paper we would have to file at the local courthouse before we left town. He then took our $20.00. I asked him if he knew any reasonable place to stay. He sure did. He sent us 'bout three miles on up in the holler to a beautiful place called Bull's Motor Court & Bar. For $25.00 a night we had a room with a bed and an overhead light bulb. It was really nice. We had TV and bathrooms in the bar and a nice creek out back if you wanted a bath. Oh, you got a free first drink in the bar as a wedding gift.

Everybody in the neighborhood heard 'bout me and Pootsie getting married and they threw us a real wedding bash. There was music and real mountain moonshine, and good food. We couldn't have found a better place. Some of them old mountain men really loved dancin' with my southern belle from down Louisiana way. After a couple of nights of honeymoonin' we left for the city courthouse. We gave the paper to the lady in the courthouse. I reckon they had to register us or somethin'. "Have either one of you been married before?" she asked. "Well of course we have - both of us - many times," we told her. "When was your divorce settled on your most recent marriage?" she asked. We looked at each other kinda puzzled. "What in the world is a *da-vorce?*" we asked.

Episode Fourteen: Grandma's Witch

It has really been difficult for me lately. I was ridin' my moped down the road and I felt something weird happenin'. Sparks started flyin' off the bottom of the frame. I stopped! The frame had bent all the way to the ground. I slowly pushed, dragged, and cussed the bike for miles to my moped mechanic. I asked him what was wrong with my junky moped. After a few minutes of hollering at me in languages I didn't know for sure, he clearly stated, "That damn bike has a weight limit of 300 pounds!" Hmm... was he trying to tell me something? Was I a tad overweight? He told me he would try and fix it, but only if I would quit torturing that #$@#* moped with my big fat ass. Ok! I think I got the picture.

I walked home. Little Lamb asked me where the family vehicle was. I didn't have the nerve to tell her that I had gotten so big that I bent the frame. I told her it was being' serviced. I went into the barn and found an old pair of stand-up feed scales. I think the old farmer that used to live here used them for cabbage, too. I weighed myself. It told me that I weighed about 460 pounds, give or take a few. Wow! No wonder Little Lamb didn't like sleepin' with me anymore. She was in real good shape. She didn't weigh a pound over 300.

I didn't have the money to get all those magic pills and weight loss plans everybody else uses, so I went to my Grandma and asked her what to do. She had moved up here in the mountains from the southern tip of Louisiana where she learned about doctorin' from the Cajun people. In fact, I think one of her old Cajun friends came up to the mountains around the same time. She lives in an old shack on up in the holler above Grandma, and I think she may know something about getting some of this weight off of me.

When I got to Grandma's, (took about all day to walk there) I told her my problem. She told me 'bout her old lady friend up the holler. Her name was Madam Morella. Grandma told me we would get a bite to eat and go up and see her. It was 'bout dark. Grandma told me things 'bout Madam Morella that kind'a scared me. She said she was from the old country and knew things - many things. She had magic! Grandma told me over and over that, "whatever you do, when we get to Madam Morella's house, do not look her directly in the eyes - never. She has power! Don't look her in the eyes, no matter what." I think Madam Morella may be a practicing witch, but who cares, if she can get this weight off.

We walked up the holler and just before we got to her shack, Grandma warned me again not to look into her eyes. I asked her why, and Grandma told me she could make any man a slave just by makin' direct eye contact with him. Yeah, sure, I thought! "Ok, Grandma, I'll not look into Madam Witch's eyes." Grandma scolded me hard for calling her a witch.

We got to the door of the old shack. There was no electricity or phone lines to the house. There was a dim glow from the window from a small cookin' type fireplace. Just before Grandma started to knock, a low scratchy voice comin' from inside stated, "Come on in; door's unlocked; always is, just come on in." Grandma went inside and I slowly followed her. "Take a seat up here near the fire; warm your bones. There's a chill in the air, yep, warm you bones," the old lady stated. I noticed Madam Morella was a little tiny woman; couldn't weigh over 90 pounds soakin' wet. She had pretty long silver hair and sat in an old rocker. Madam Morella said, "So someone's wantin' to get rid of some weight; yep, lot of weight; yep, I know how to get it off. What do you call yourself?" This was definitely scary. I hadn't even told this woman my name, and she already knew what I was there for. "That's me, my name is Max! Yeah, I need to lose a few pounds." Madam Morella responded with laughter and exclaimed, "A few pounds my beeehind! You need to lose a hundred at least, maybe two. I can fix you good. Look over here at me." (I remember what Grandma warned, so I was careful not to look into her eyes). She told me how she would prepare a nasty tastin' brew and how I would have to take one level cupful every two hours, all day, until it was all gone. She told me that I had to follow these simple instructions to the letter. If I missed a dose or took it anytime except exactly two hours apart, it would not work. I asked her how much it would cost, and she told me I could bring her a sack of taters (good ones) for payment sometime when I was up her way. I agreed and shook her hand.

She began making my get-thin cure with a large half-gallon mason jar. She poured in three-fourths full of something I believe was moonshine. She told me that this was medicinal grade alcohol and would help dissolve and deliver the herbs she was about to put in. She called it a tincture. She also warned me to keep it away from open flames. She added a handful of herbs and spoke some words I didn't understand and began a little chant. She then stirred the mixture in the jar. She spoke a few more words and raised her voice with some kind of eerie chanting. She then added several magic ingredients from small bottles. This stuff looked and smelled real nasty. She stirred it up again, stuck her finger in and tasted it. "'Bout right," she stated. She then rubbed a little of the potion on my forehead. "This will get the job done, but you have to take one level cupful every two hours, all day, until the entire half-gallon is gone. Best if you shake it gently each time before you use it, too." I asked her, "What should I eat, and what can I eat?" She told me to eat anything I wanted, all I wanted, as often as I wanted to eat, and then she smiled at me.

We visited for a little while longer, then Grandma and I left for the night, me with one half-gallon of prime 190 proof fat remover from Madam Morella. I decided to start takin' the potion early the next morning'. I woke up at 5am and took my first cupful. Wow! This stuff was strong - it burnt going down, and it was bitter as gall. After one cup, I could hardly stand up. My head was buzzin' and I was very happy. I laid back down and in 'bout ten minutes, it hit. I had to run to the bathroom. It was bad! When finished, I went back to bed, and in 'bout another ten minutes, back to the bathroom. Finally, after checking the clock the second hour came, and I drank another cupful. Ten minutes later, again, I was in the bathroom. Little Lamb ran me and my potion out of the house. Thank goodness there was an old outhouse and hay-filled 'backer barn to rest in. By the third cup, (full level cup, 190 proof) I could barely make it to the outhouse; no way I could eat anything. I made it through the 5pm dose, only one more to go and it will all be over with. The outhouse and hay bed in the barn had pretty much become one in the same place. I was spinning so bad it was all I could do to take that last cupful. I think I went to sleep or something shortly after that.

I slept for three days in that barn. When I awoke at daybreak, I felt strange and different. I went to the creek and took a bath. I knew I stunk something terrible bad. That morning, when I walked in the house, I smelled Little Lamb's fine biscuits and gravy and side meat cooking, but I just could not eat. I had no desire for food. I told Little Lamb 'bout my whole ordeal, and she laughed at me. "Any idiot that would drink a half-gallon of 'shine in one day is lucky to be alive." Then she got mad. "What did you have to pay for that 'shine?" "It was not 'shine - it was fat-burning potion," I told her. "Sure it was!" she exclaimed. I told her that the potion cost me nothing but a sack of taters. "Oh, that's right. I need to take Madam Morella a sack of taters."

I went into the barn and weighed myself on those old scales. I was down to 390 pounds. In three days, I had lost 70 pounds. This thing worked quick, but would it last? I sacked up some good taters and began the walk to Madam Morella's shack; took most of the day. I got there in the late afternoon. She thanked me for the taters and asked if I would mind choppin' some wood. It would help with the weight loss. I told her, "Sure!" I ended up staying the night. Five or seven days later, (I'm not sure) I was still at Madam Morella's shack. The time had completely slipped by. I was still losing weight. Grandma walked up the path to where I was finishing replacing the roof on Madam's shack. "What are you up to, boy?" she asked. "Oh, I've been helping out this old lady, and you are right! She's not a witch! I have cut her firewood, painted her shack, cleaned out the well, and been working today on re-boarding this old roof," I told Grandma. "How long you been up here, boy?" asked Grandma. "I think 'bout five or seven days. Why do you ask?" I responded. Grandma looked at me, grinned, shook her head and stated, "Went and looked into her eyes, didn't ya, boy?"

Episode Fifteen: Selling Teeth

I've been hiding out; I mean staying in southern Louisiana for a while. I'm back in the Blue Ridge now and glad to be back. Flat broke! Moped's out of gas! Sweetie's real mad. Been hot in that two-room tent but staying on the New River has its advantages. Fair fishing and cool skinny dipping are just fine on a hot day. Jobs are scarce and it's getting about time to scrounge up some money.

I been watching the price of gold and it's getting high enough that I decided to sell my 18 gold teeth. Somebody told me that gold teeth were bringing $70 or $80 each. Wow! I can get a cheap room for a month or two, gas for my moped, a gift for my Sweetie, and take a trip to the drive-thru for some burgers and stuff. I had no idea what I was in for. My first problem was to find someone to sell them to. Someone at the campground told me about a good place to sell gold in town, so, I started on the 12-mile trip to town, teeth in tow. I finally got to the gold buying place and the guy who buys wouldn't be in until the next day. So, back to the campground I walked. The next morning, I got up early and headed off to the gold place. I finally got there and asked the gold man how much he paid for gold teeth. He asked to see them, and I cracked the biggest open mouth smile I could muster and showed him all 18 of them. "Hmm…," he muttered. "You'll have to get them out of your mouth so I can test them." "How do I get them out?" I asked. "I guess you should go to a dentist," he told me. Well, that's out. I asked him what gold teeth were bringing, and he told me real gold teeth could be from 14k to 22k; bring anywhere from $60 to $200 each. Wow! That's a potential $3,600. "Do you pay cash?" "Sure do! Just need proper ID when you sell them." He also told me they needed to be clean and dry with a little slick laugh. Ok. I made an appointment for the following week. He thanked me, and I proceeded to walk back to the campground.

Three thousand, six hundred dollars… Hmm… that's a lot of teeth money. Should I tell Sweetie? No way. I wouldn't make it through the first night. Once I fell into a deep snore; Sweetie, a butcher knife, and well, you get the picture. "So how do I get these teeth out without Sweetie knowing?" I thought as I walked. It would come to me. My buddy Joe at the campground was good at fixing things. He fixed my moped a couple of times, several leaks in the tent, and sewed up a bad cut I got with the hatchet when cutting kindling for the cook fire. Yep! Joe was the way to go. I eased in the back way to Joe's camper and told him I had decided to get false teeth, but I had to pull out my teeth starting with the metal ones first. I asked him if he would pull them out for me. "What?" he asked me. "Yeah, I think I want to get me some false teeth. If you can get these metals ones out, I'll let her heal and then maybe you can pull the rest out." He looked at my teeth and told me that it was probably a good idea with all those cavities. "Cavities!" What the heck. Oh, well. "Get 'em out, Joe!" After a few hours of liquid pain killing and discussing the world's problems, Joe was ready to pull my gold teeth and I was, too. After a quart or two of Joe's 'shine, I was ready to let him pull them all. Little Joey (Joe's boy) ran by two or three times and told me little Sweetie was looking for me. "Whatever you do, don't tell her where I'm at or what I'm doing."

I don't think Joe had any idea that I intended to sell my gold teeth. I had no idea what a night I was in for. At about 9 pm, flashlight, 'shine, and vice grips in hand, Joe started by putting his arm on my forehead and clamping those vice grips on one of my teeth. I was actually laughing at first. He started wrenching, and twisting, and tugging, and pulling, and cussing. I was sweating, and finally out she came, blood squirting everywhere. "Dang it, Joe, that's not a metal tooth." "What difference does it make?" "It makes all the difference… get a metal one next time!" "Ok, Max. Here goes!" After drinking a little more pain killer, I told Joe to give me some more. He did, and he latched onto another tooth. Whew! Out she came. It was a shiny (red) gold tooth. "Now, Joe, get the other 17 out." Nineteen teeth and four hours later, (the flashlight batteries run down), I was an almost dead but happy man. Just a walk back to town and I was in the money. I wasn't sure how much blood I lost, but I had to be close to unconscious. I wobbled back to my tent and Sweetie was in a real tither. "Where you been? Who you been with? What have you been doing? Why you got blood all over you?" "It was terrible Sweetie. I was walking home, and a bunch of thugs jumped me on the road and beat me up. Lost half my teeth. Took a real beating, but I'll find 'em. You can be sure of that." Sweetie got to feeling real sorry for me and made me an ice pack from the camp store ice machine. I really needed that ice, the swelling was real bad. I carefully hid my gold teeth and passed out on the cot.

I didn't wake up until afternoon the next day. I was in a real bad way. I was in the most pain I had ever been in. My mouth was swollen shut, couldn't talk; (Sweetie seemed to like that). I was surely running a fever. I was real sick. The camp host offered to take me to the local hospital emergency room. I went, and they put somewhere in the neighborhood of thirty stitches in my mouth, gave me some antibiotics and high-powered pain killers, and sent me on my way. I didn't have insurance or money. I think they put me on the easy payment plan. After a few pain killers, I slept for most of the next three days. When I finally woke up, I was feeling some better, but still in a lot of pain. That doc told me that I would probably get really infected. Oh, well. Three thousand six hundred dollars was worth a little pain. And no one knew but me. I had an appointment the next day at the gold place. I got my teeth out of hiding and carefully washed off all the blood. The next morning, I headed to town. When I got to the gold place, I had to wait in line; two were ahead of me. The best I could understand, gold had shot up to over $1,800 an ounce. Wow! My teeth could be worth $4,000... maybe more; who knows?

Finally, after about an hour, I got to sit down with the gold man. After a bit of friendly chitchat, he took my bag of teeth. He kept staring at me, and finally asked, "How did you get these out so quick? I can't even get a dentist appointment in under four months." I told him how me, my friend Joe, and our brother 'shine, got 'em out of there in record time. He kind of gritted his teeth, shook his head, then laughed a little. He took a pair of needle-nose pliers and pulled out one of the gold teeth, looked it over, rubbed it on some kind of stone, and put a few drops of something on it. After a few seconds, he dropped the tooth back into the bag, looked over the others, and asked me where I got my teeth capped at. I told him I got them at the Southside Free Dental Clinic. He asked me if I had to pay anything for the caps, and I told him, "Not a dime!" Then he told me, "Buddy, these teeth are not gold… SORRY!!!"

Episode Sixteen: A New Diet Plan

So, after all my divorces, I was beginning to ponder a way to feel attractive again (to females, of course) without going anywhere near Grandma and her pet witch Madam Morella. It took me nearly two years to break that spell, but I did loose down to normal weight. I had managed to put on some extra pounds, so they had to go before I go a courting. I had always heard of all those weight-loss secrets and fancy diet plans, but never had no need to try 'em. But, being alone now for two months, I thought I might start looking around and reading up on some simple plan to lose weight besides witchcraft.

I was sittin' at home one evening, and it came across the tube. It was strange, like someone knew I needed to see that commercial; it was just what ol' Max was lookin' for! A simple way to lose some weight! All I had to do was call this phone number and they would send everything I needed straight to my house... That seemed easy enough! They had three different programs I could pick from: 3-day/10-pound weight loss, 6-day/20-pound weight loss, or the 7-day/50-pound program. I thought I would order the simple 3-day program and see how it worked.

So, I got the phone and started dialing! This real nice man answered, "Easy to Lose Weight Loss, how may I help you?"

"I need to order your 3-day/10-pound program please." He told me the total, asked how I would be paying, and then my shipping address. After I gave him all the information he needed, he said that it would ship that day and I could expect it the next day. Wow! I was excited. Seemed like a great company, so I was guessing their program would be the same.

The next day, I was messing around the house, and I heard a knock at the door. Hmm...wonder if that's my weight loss stuff?! Sure enough, I answered the door and there before me was this appealing, athletic, 19-year-old babe. She was dressed in some kind of tight shorts with a sign hanging around her neck. I was almost speechless, but somehow, I seemed to stutter out "hello" and asked her if I could help her. She said she was a representative of the weight loss program I had ordered. I began reading the sign hanging around her neck, "If you can catch me, you can have me!" Hmm… without a second thought, I darted out the door after her. We ran for miles (or at least seemed like it), and finally, I gave up. I was huffin' and puffin' and gaspin' for breath! And, my little woman was out of sight. Oh well, I thought, better luck next time. So, I wandered back home. After a relaxing evening and soothing my aching muscles, I managed to lay down. The next day, Wednesday to be exact, the same lady showed up at my door, and it was a repeat of the previous day. I was finally beginning to catch on to this process...the more I chase this "babe", the more weight I will lose! This should be easy… day two gone, and one more to go. So, the next day, I went through the same process… and man I was feeling great. I had already lost 10 pounds! I was going to be a "hunk" when this was done. I still couldn't catch her...but I had lost the weight that was promised.

So, I pulled out the mailing insert, and gave the number a call, again. I wanted to try the 6-day/20-pound program. The man answered, and I ordered the program. It arrived the next morning. When I answered the door, I was amazed. There before me stood the most beautiful, amazing woman I had ever seen! She had on some real nice running shoes and nothing else except a sign! It read the same thing as my first weight loss representative. Well… I'm out the door like a shot! She's mine, mine… A-L-L... mine! After about 2 miles of running, I was beginning to realize this woman was in great shape! I tried my hardest, but no luck… I'm never gonna catch her! So, my next four days involved the same thing, every day! But I could tell that I was getting in better shape each day! I was gaining ground! I promised myself that if I had lost the 20 pounds I paid for, I would be delighted to give them one more try! So, I weighed myself on the sixth day, and to my surprise, I had lost 20 pounds. I was feelin' great and lookin' good! At this point I realized I had nothing to lose, so I called them back and ordered the 7-day/50-pound program. The person kept asking me if I was sure that I wanted to give that program a try; he said it was their hardest program. But there was no doubt in my mind! I told him absolutely! I hadn't felt this good in years! So, he said it would be shipped.

That night I was so anxious I couldn't even sleep! I thought I would surprise the lady on the other side of the door the next morning, by being ready to go as soon as the knock came! If I could get out the door quicker, I might have a chance of catching her! So, I paced the floor all night, and at daybreak, I was ready to run! The knock came, same time as the previous orders. And, man was I ready! Had my running shorts and shoes on. I even had a bottle of water ready to go! I crept to the door...swung it open… and there stood this 7-foot-tall, muscle bulging guy! I was surprised… all he had on was a pink pair of running shoes and a sign around his neck. What in the world? This guy

must be lost! My eyes wandered to the sign and it read,
"If I catch you, you are ALL…mine!!!"

I took off running through the house, out the
back door, and my 7 days was on! I ran the whole 7
days and never stopped! There was no way I was
letting this guy catch me… and I never seen him
again!

I lost 65 pounds that week! No more weight loss
for Max. I'm going to be happy with me and who I
am, regardless of what any woman thinks. Time for a
pizza!

Episode Seventeen: Ask Max

Hi, it's Max! I get a lot of cards and letters from many of you fine readers asking me advice on all kinds of things, so I thought I'd try to give my two cents worth to a few of those questions! Here goes.

DEAR MAX: Have you ever tried running fluid in your moped tires? I thought it might make them stick to the road better and increase the amount of weight we could haul. What do you think?
MOPED GLIDER

DEAR MOPED GLIDER: Sure have! Got 'em filled up at the local tractor place. Made it all the way to town with sweetie number two til the front tire exploded on a rock in the road. Might try better tires next time. P.S. Sweetie liked to drown right before she fell off.

DEAR MAX: Wondering if you could help me out? The best I can tell, you've been married or almost married over seven times. Does it ever get any easier breaking up?
LONELY BREAKING HEART

DEAR LONELY BREAKING HEART: It depends on how fast the moped's goin' when you break up!

DEAR MAX: Considering you've had so much experience with the women in your day, maybe you could help me gather some ideas for a present for my wife for our one-year anniversary. Any suggestions?
MARRIED AND CONFUSED

DEAR MARRIED AND CONFUSED: You sure are! You mean we have to buy something for 'em? Let's see, first year of marriage… Oh! It's always good to get the kids some toys so you'll have some alone time with little honey lamb. Oh! I know another good gift. Cheap jewelry from your local flea market will keep her around for at least six more months.

MAX: You bein' a fancy writer and all, I'd like to know how many years you went to school.
DESIRING TO LEARN

DEAR DESIRING: For your info, I spent almost 18 years in school. They finally graduated me from the sixth grade and told me to get off their property 'cause I kept gettin' stuck in the little chairs in the lunchroom, and I kept being mistaken for the teacher by the small kids.

DEAR MAX: I'm 39 and very beautiful, currently single, a tad bit overweight, and lookin' for a man (Hint! Hint!) I just have one question for you. Do you have any prejudice against certain types of women?
LOOKIN'

DEAR LOOKIN': No, I love all women equally. Still currently happily married, but as soon as she leaves, I'll be in touch.

DEAR MAX: You're a man, right? Maybe you can help me with my husband. He's gone all the time, whether it's deer hunting, fishing, or just "off to the grocery store". I just want him home at least a couple hours of the evening. Any suggestions?
HOME ALL ALONE

DEAR HOME ALL ALONE: I'm a REAL man, and I know exactly what to do! One, get your hunting and fishing license and start going hunting and fishing, but not with him. You don't really need a fishing pole or gun, just make the effort of going without him. (Still currently happily married, but as soon as she leaves, I'll be in touch.)

HI MAX: My name is Sally. I'm a little too young for you, just a few days over 17, so I thought I'd go for a younger Fetterbrush. Will you tell one of your boys that I'm interested?
FUTURE MRS. FETTERBRUSH JR.

DEAR FUTURE MRS. FETTERBRUSH: Ahh, ain't none of them boys worth a hoot. After about another 4 or 5 marriages (or 4 years, whichever comes first), I'll be in touch!

HI MAX: Valentine's Day will be here soon, and I'm stumped when it comes to all that fancy stuff. Do you have any advice on where to take your lady for this fine occasion?
NOT SO ROMANTIC

DEAR NOT SO ROMANTIC: You shouldn't have to worry about all that wine 'n dine mess... All you need is a bucket of chicken and a two-dollar bottle of wine. Your lady should be thankful you did anything at all!

DEAR MAX: I don't like the way you present women in your articles. All women deserve respect from the opposite sex.

DOWN ON MAX

DEAR DOWN ON MAX: I agree fully, so what's your question and phone number?

DEAR MAX: I have no clue what to get the love of my life for Valentine's Day. He always buys me beautiful roses, chocolates, and a nice dinner. Any suggestions for a good man?
NEED SUGGESTIONS

DEAR NEED SUGGESTIONS: Don't buy him nothing. It'll make him appreciate you better. P.S. If you need someone to share those chocolates with, just give me a call!

DEAR MAX: I got a lot of junk for Christmas I don't like, but the guy at the flea market wouldn't take it back. Any suggestions?
JUNK FOR CHRISTMAS

DEAR JUNK FOR CHRISTMAS: Just remember who give you all them presents. Re-wrap 'em and give 'em back to who they came from next year; not like they'll remember anyways.

DEAR MAX: I was going around a curve on my moped and my twelve-pack of can drinks started flying off the floorboard. As I reached for 'em, I run my moped square off the road, down a bank, into a tree and totaled it. Shouldn't the company who made the twelve-pack be liable?
TOTALED BY A TWELVE-PACK

DEAR TOTALED BY A TWELVE-PACK: I'm not an attorney, but I think it depends totally on the number of cans that were empty. Oh! Did you manage to save the rest of that twelve-pack?

DEAR MAX: My dear uncle passed away and I recently found out he left me $10,000 in cash. I've lived by my wits all my life, barely making it from week-to-week. Not sure how to proceed with spending the money. Any suggestions?
MADGE WITH TEN-GRAND TO SPEND

DEAR MADGE: Call me! (Seriously, call me now!) Don't wait, Call!

HI MAX: My daughter's birthday is coming up and she expects some kind of big celebration for this occasion. I'm a little short on cash, but I'd still like to surprise her. Any advice for an inexpensive birthday party?

DAD LOW ON CASH

DEAR LOW ON CASH: They have really cool dances at most rest homes every Friday and Saturday night. It's free and the food's good. Just tell 'em it's grandma's birthday!

DEAR MAX: I've been having some troubles at work. I never get noticed by my co-workers, no matter what I do. How do you think I can get some respect in the workplace?

UNAPPRECIATED

DEAR UNAPPRECIATED: Don't let it get you down. Just don't take a bath for about two weeks. Trust me, nobody will be able to ignore you then. You'll definitely get the attention you deserve!

DEAR MAX: My 20-year-old son lives with me and my husband. I don't want to upset him, but he needs to get out and get a place of his own. Do you have any suggestions to motivate him without hurting him?

FRUSTRATED MAMA

DEAR FRUSTRATED: It's quite simple really. Stop feeding him; give him no money; stop washing his clothes; change the locks; rent his room out. If none of the above works, just turn him into the sheriff. He's probably doing something illegal anyway if he's that old and still living at home.

HI MAX: I have been trying to help my son with his science project for school; but it's been so long since I was in school, I'm lost on how to get started. Any suggestions on a science project topic?
DAD WITHOUT A CLUE

DEAR WITHOUT A CLUE: The kind of projects I'd come up with are probably not allowed. Just hire a kid from last year who passed and use their project. Be sure to change the name to your kid's name.

DEAR MAX: My sweetie of six months has a birthday coming up soon and I am stumped on what to buy her. She loves fancy china and things like that, but I am on a tight budget these days. Any suggestions on a gift?
LOW BUDGET BOYFRIEND

DEAR LOW BUDGET: Get her an old gallon pottery liquor jug (about a dollar at a junk store) and fill it with gas for the moped. Also, get her a six-pack for her nerves so she won't accidentally drink gas out of the jug!

DEAR MAX: My sister is having a baby in a couple of months and I still haven't bought her a baby shower gift. I'm a man. Men don't do that kind of thing, but I know I'll hear it if I don't get her some little something. Any suggestions?
BABY SHOWER GUY

DEAR BABY SHOWER GUY: A can of gas for her moped. (She'll need it to get to the hospital!)

HEY MAX: You being such a clever man, I was wondering if you could help me think of a name for our new little puppy. He is a dark brown Pitbull. Any suggestions?
PITBULL OWNER

DEAR PITBULL OWNER: Name it Honey Lamb. That way you only have one name to holler when you need the dog or the woman.

DEAR MAX: What's the fastest way to get to Southern Louisiana? Been wanting to do some fishing down there.

RATHER BE FISHING

DEAR RATHER BE FISHING: By moped.

DEAR MAX: I've been trying to lose weight. I weigh over 300 pounds and I think my man's about to throw me out of the house. Any suggestions?
WEIGHT WATCHER GIRL

DEAR WEIGHT WATCHER GIRL: Give me a call. I'm keeping my eye out for another Mrs. Fetterbrush. So why do you need to lose weight?

DEAR MAX: My old lady dyed her hair red, it just doesn't look right on her. Any suggestions?
RED'S GOT TO GO

DEAR RED'S GOT TO GO: Spray paint - dollar store!

Episode Eighteen: Aunt Fezze

My Aunt Fezzelinnas Fetterbrush passed away in Louisiana last month. I didn't want to write about it, but the whole mess has been weighing heavy on my mind, so I guess I better get it off my chest. It all started with a phone call from my cousin Mistral Fetterbrush (he was a Fetterbrush on my momma's side). He informed me that our Aunt Fezzelinnas (we just called her Fezze for short) had passed on. She was 96 years old and had no immediate living family. She had told Mistral to be sure and have her buried in the little family cemetery in the Blue Ridge Mountains. So, Mistral informed us that he and some of our other cousins had built a large plywood box for Aunt Fezze and had sent her our way by a rental truck with instructions for her burial. You see, the last time I saw Aunt Fezze, she weighed in at just over 490 pounds. That's the reason my cousins had to build a special box. There were just no caskets big enough for Aunt Fezze; and I'm sure my cousins had very little money. Cousin Mistral told me good luck and hung up.

As I was pondering that phone call, I heard what sounded like a truck pull up in the driveway. It was a $39.95 a night rental truck. Out came cousin Bernie and Cousin Jessie. "Hi Max; good to see you old buddy!" one of them hollered. I thought for a minute and asked them, "How long you all been on the road?" "'Bout 23 hours counting the stop-over at the state line dance show!" exclaimed Jessie. "You got Fezze in back of that truck?" I asked. "Sure do." "Wouldn't she be smelling by now?" "No, we packed ice bags around her, but she's not going to hold much longer." stated Bernie. "Gotta get her in the ground soon."

They opened up the back of that rental truck and there sat a big plywood box that looked more like a shipping container than a casket. "Don't open that box!" stated Jessie. You won't like want you see." "And smell!" exclaimed Bernie with a, "ha ha." "Gotta get her in the ground soon. You know where this cemetery is Max?" On top of the box was a stapled-on paper that had specific instructions and directions on how to get to this small cemetery in the Blue Ridge.

I wasn't sure about the laws in North Carolina or Louisiana about funerals, but I was sure something probably wasn't exactly legal about how my cousins were handling Aunt Fezze's funeral. I called up some friends and asked them if they would meet me at the old road that took us up the mountain to the old cemetery. I asked them to bring some shovels to help dig a grave. Most agreed, and we headed off. We drove the rental truck to the entrance to the old road leading up the mountain to the cemetery. We waited for my friends to show up and we all piled in that rental truck and started the long, slow trip up that old mountain road. That old rental truck impressed me. Them dual wheels pulled us right up that mountain.

We finally got to the old partially fenced-in cemetery. It was all grown up and unmaintained. We got out and started looking around. There was really Fetterbrushes buried there. It was amazing. I didn't even know Fetterbrushes had been here in the mountains before me. It was a real nice feeling. We started slowly digging on a spot we didn't think anybody else was buried in. It was slow, hot, hard work. That cemetery was on a steep knob that apparently grew rocks. Those small shovels were no match for those rocks. We had worked in the hot sun for an hour and our hole was no more than two-foot deep. This was going to take some time. My friends were already complaining and wanting to back out.

We decided the truck was getting too hot for Aunt Fezze, so we decided to move her out of the truck into the shade. They had nailed her to the floor of the rental truck to keep her from sliding around in the truck during shipping from Louisiana. We worked for another hour breaking her loose from the floor of that truck. My cousin Mistral had built a really nice box for Fezze. It had really cool hand grips. We slowly lifted her and walked her down the loading ramp and started heading toward the big oak shade tree, and suddenly there was a crack, a snap, a ker-plump, and the bottom of that big box fell right to the ground and so did Aunt Fezze. No faster than she hit the ground (it was steep), she slowly began to roll; and roll she did. Right under our feet she went, taking us down; down the steep grade she rolled. Bump, bump, bump; picking up speed right through the outer fence of the cemetery. It finally clicked in our brains that Aunt Fezze was rolling away. We dropped the 200-lb box that our cousin Mistral had half-built and began to chase Aunt Fezze. We heard her crashing through the woods, and she was apparently picking up speed. Ker-plump! Ker-plump! Limbs and small trees were snapping. We commenced to running. About 50 yards passed the outer cemetery fence was another fence that had "No Trespassing" signs posted every ten feet. She had busted right through that, too. We looked and the grade became steeper. We went from running to sliding down a real steep bank. There was a real nice path created by Fezze. Finally, we could see that her big body had come to a stop right at the top of what looked to be a rock cliff. Just as we almost had her in reach, over she went. It was quiet for a few seconds as we arrived at the edge. We looked over the edge and saw her body as it made a huge splash into the river at the bottom of that cliff.

Wow! Soaking wet from the tidal wave that crested above the cliff's edge created by poor Aunt Fezze's drop, we decided to climb the long steep grade back up to the cemetery and think everything over a bit. We got back to the casket and noticed big gallon plastic bags full of some green-looking stuff laying all around where Aunt Fezze fell out. Apparently, these bags had been stuffed around Fezze. About that time, everything really went from bad to terrible. Someone in the woods shouted through something like a megaphone "Freeze - it's the Law - you're all under arrest!" We just stood there, looking dumb, and slowly raised our arms, as we were used to when we heard such a statement. About six or seven armed officers with badges circled around us and arrested us. They confiscated the green bags of whatever and put us all in the back of that rental truck and took us back to town for processing.

As we went to town, my other cousins were telling me how this had all been planned by our cousin Mistral and that he probably had planned for someone in the mountain to dig up Aunt Fezze in the middle of the night to get those bags. It took most of the day at the jail, but as it turned out, Mistral worked at a big factory that bottled herbs and seasonings. He had used a batch of old thyme or something the company gave him to pack Aunt Fezze in to keep her stable and to soak up any moisture from the melting ice packs (kind of like packing peanuts). The law had been called by some suspicious neighbor who seen us taking that rental truck up the old cemetery road. Naturally, the law had to investigate. When they saw those big plastic bags laying around, they became suspicious, too. After the law had talked to Cousin Mistral, we were all cleared, and finally, all got released. As we were walking out of the jail, Cousin Jessie asked, "What about Aunt Fezze?"

Episode Nineteen: Burger Slinging Max

Well, I might as well admit I have been real lazy, not having a real job for, let's see, 'bout 23 years. I decided it's time for Max to get back to work. I went home to Louisiana where I was raised and started looking for a job. I figured it would be easier to find a job where people knew me, and it should be a lot easier in the big city than in the Blue Ridge. After a few weeks of looking, it suddenly occurred to me that no one wanted to hire poor old Max. "What was I good at?" they asked. "Well, I was good at fishing, and mopedding, and hunting, and eating (really good at eating), and oh, I guess I'm an expert at love." Those answers didn't seem to help much. All the jobs I wanted were already taken. They even about called the law on me when I tried to get hired on as a part-time preacher at one of the parish churches. (The sign said "souls wanted" - I would have settled for Deacon. I don't think they liked my old rundown moped.

As I went from place to place, I noticed all the fast food stores had "Now Hiring" signs on the windows. Ok! It's time for Max to do fast food. I walked into the first one and exclaimed, "I'm here!" Some young sickly little boy asked me what I wanted, and I told him, "I want a job." He (the manager) pretty much hired me on the spot, but I had to fill out a lot of papers and take several tests including a drug test that I passed with flying colors. After a few days they had me come in at 4 am. I was actually staying about three miles away from this place, so the moped did ok getting me there in the morning. The first day was fun and exciting. I had never worked in fast food before (and I was making minimum wage, whatever that is).

They did what I think they called "intensive new-hire training" on me the first week. They put me with all these little kids to train me. You see, I was the "old man on board" to these teenagers. But I know things they don't, and I'll get into that later. The first week they let me do just about everything. I made milkshakes, flipped burgers, (mostly in the floor), cooked fries, swept, cleaned, swept some more, emptied the trash, cleaned the bathrooms. I guess my first real mess-up was in the ladies' bathroom. I forgot to put the cleaning sign up, plus I forgot which bathroom I was in, and the wrong woman walked in. Yeah, this crazy woman came in and without giving me warning, took one look at me, and just totally flipped out. Yeah, she started screaming something about a pervert in the women's bathroom; and yeah, the place was packed with people; and yeah, the big cheese regional manager from corporate was visiting; and yeah, the cops arrived; and yeah, I begged forgiveness to the customer (and my boss, and the cops), explaining to her that I was almost blind and could not read signs very well. The young visiting corporate big wheel felt sorry for me and gave me a raise. I think they got a kickback from the government for hiring almost blind people who could not read very well and had been trained to cook in prison.

The same day I was promoted to full-fledged "assistant cook's helper". My job was to clean the stove. All that cleaning junk they provided never really got the stove clean, so I made up my own cleaning solution from home. I found a good hiding place at work for my magic solution. It worked faster and no one ever knew how I got the stove clean so much quicker than other assistant cook's helpers. Before long, I was assistant cook. They moved someone from bathroom cleaning to my old position. The stove cleaning job slowed down very much after I moved up. The big wheels from corporate came in to learn why my stove cleaning was so much faster than their normal methods. I told them I invented a new cleaner that worked much faster. They told me to keep it quiet. I got a raise and a "Most Creative Employee of the Year" award. The big wheels took a sample of my new cleaner and left.

The burgers I was cooking tasted like every other frozen fast-cooked burger that had been warmed up in a contraption that they called the "express burger machine". I knew it wasn't anything but a fancy microwave with a few light bulbs. I had to come up with something to make me look good to the customers while I was working so they would brag on me to management. My goal was to get to that front counter, and eventually management. One night at home, under a full moon at just the stroke of midnight, I mixed and tasted, and mixed and tasted some more, until finally success. The secret mixture was salty with a touch of sweet, slightly hot, with a little magic spice. This would be a perfect seasoning for use on these bread burgers when I was cooking, but no one at the restaurant could know what I was doing. I mixed up a big bag and left for work the next morning at 10 am.

The next day, I started slowly sprinkling my new secret seasoning on the burgers and added a little extra liquid smoke juice (the smoke odor went out the vent over the highway and drove passersby crazy for our handmade microwave burgers) and I added extra cooking oil to give them a little more flavor. It worked! The first day, our "suggestion box" filled up with comments like *"the burgers were especially good today… would love to know your secret"*, and many other great comments. The management had to ship these on to corporate every other day. When I didn't work, the comment box was empty. When I cooked, it filled up with great comments. In about two weeks, the big cheese showed up from corporate, and this time some of the big wheels from the corporate headquarters came along. They wanted to know what I was doing differently from all the other cooks. I told them about adding a little extra smoke and oil and about my secret spice I was trying on the burgers. The people from headquarters didn't smile when I told them I was adding things to their burgers. They just took a sample of my spice with them and told me to keep it quiet for now.

In a few days, I was moved to the drive-thru register and given another raise for no apparent reason. It had come down from corporate management. I loved the drive-thru; it was really hectic at times, though. I had to come up with another idea to increase my customer appeal now that I was at the drive-thru. I went to the grocery store and got several bags of Hershey's® Kisses® and started sneaking a couple in every bag. I kept them hid in my pocket, so the other employees didn't have a clue what I was doing. After a few days, people would pull up to the drive-thru and if I wasn't working, they would just *"drive through"*. Yep! Another visit from the big cheese at corporate. This time somebody they called the Regional Vice-President of the company came in. I had to tell them (without anyone else listening) why my drive-thru customers were much happier with me than all the other drive-thru associates. I told them about the candy, and they told me to keep it quiet. I got another raise and was moved to front register and made an "assistant customer support manager". Wasn't quite sure what that meant, but it looked good on paper.

To keep the whole thing going, I secretly bought some of the restaurants $1.00 gift certificates as I could afford it and passed these out to some of my best register customers (on the sly, of course) and you bet my lines started to increase. When I wasn't busy, I would walk out into the dining room and check on my best customers, asking them if I could bring them anything else or if their food was cooked to their satisfaction. Some complained that the burgers were better when I cooked them, but most were very happy with my service. After a few weeks of handing out $1.00 gift certificates, many of our customers would not let anyone else serve them but me. Guess what? The big cheese rolled in with the chain's Vice President. Wow! I had the attention of the VP of the company. I explained what I had done, expecting a raise and move to management, but to my surprise I was given an offer. Apparently, their scientist liked my cleaning solution (corporate said their testing proved it was safe and environmentally friendly, too) and my special seasoning (none of them had ever thought of putting this special mixture together for a burger). They offered me $1,000 to sell my cleaning and seasoning recipes to them. All I had to do was to sign several pages of paperwork. I agreed and got my $1,000 check ($756.35 after withholding). They never asked me for the lists of ingredients. I guess their scientist figured it all out.

Three days later they fired me for "endangering the public for using untested cleaning solutions on cooking surfaces"; "using foodstuffs unapproved by the FDA on their burgers"; "distributing food not approved by the management"; "unauthorized use of company gift certificates"; "working in the dining room when untrained and unauthorized to do so"; "failing to put up *Bathroom Closed* signs when cleaning the bathroom"; AND "lying on my application". . .(not sure what that was about!)

I asked the restaurant manager what I had done wrong. He told me that the truth is that, "You were just too good to our customers. They were accustomed to being treated very badly; they were perfectly happy eating the junky food we serve with no flavor; they were fine with never receiving gifts for being good customers or being asked how the service was; the fact is, if we let you get by with that, I will have to try and find other employees that will do the same... and corporate would have to find better employees for the whole chain. It's just not going to happen. And you were obviously after my job. Sorry! Oh, and for all practical purposes, you did get caught in the women's bathroom. Did I tell you the woman is an attorney's wife? I think she's going to sue you." He also told me to have a good life and stay off of their property . . . FOREVER! The best I can figure out, I was fired for doing my job too well.

Well, that's ok. I cashed my $756.35 check and my last paycheck, upgraded my moped, and went on a long-moped ride in the Louisiana countryside. I took a sleeping bag and slept out under the skies for a few weeks to ponder what had just happened to me. After much reflecting, I returned to the city and passed by the restaurant I no longer worked at (properly giving them the finger of contempt), and while looking at their windows and wobbling along on my new moped, I noticed big signs in their windows that read, "NEW SECRET SEASONING..." couldn't make the rest out. Hmm!! When I got home, I opened up a newspaper, and there was a full-page ad for the place I just got fired from stating: "All New Environmentally

Friendly Grill Cleaning Methods – and New Secret Seasoning That Makes Your Burger Taste like Heaven". Oh well; might as well laugh about it. Did I mention that my cleaning fluid was two parts paint remover and one part kerosene, and five parts carburetor cleaner, and two parts. . . and my secret seasoning was ten parts hardwood sawdust, and… oh, well, I signed papers not to divulge those secret ingredients.

I applied at another fast-food restaurant the next day (their most hated competitors, I think) and when asked about my qualifications, I told them I knew nothing, was ignorant and stupid, couldn't read or write, was mostly blind and dumb, could never have a driver's license, had a record, was an ex-con, and could never own a gun, but I would be their slave. Got hired on the spot as Assistant Cook at $15.00 per hour - Start Today! I will be Manager soon! ENJOY! From Max the Burger Master! (PS: I really don't have a record, nor am I an ex con. I just thought it would look good on my application.)

Episode Twenty: Secret Job-Hunting Tips

Thought I would tell you about some of my job hunting adventures in years past. The economy was shot, at least where I lived and everybody around, including me, needed money, so I decided to go out and seek a job. I asked over 134 potential employers for a job over a two-week period. I was hired three times by five different employers, made $112, walked out on two jobs, got fired from one, and never showed up for the rest. I learned that anybody needing work could probably find work anytime they wanted to, even in a bad economy. So instead of telling you about my jobs from the past, I am going to tell you how to land a job, anytime, anywhere, the Fetterbrush way.

Secret Job-Hunting Tip 1

Never take a bath before going to an interview. When you are sitting in a crowd of people who have suits and smelly cologne on, you will be sure and be noticed first (i.e. Stand out from the crowd). (Oh, and never brush your teeth and for goodness sake, don't use mouthwash). You don't want your interviewer to get too close to ya!

Secret Job-Hunting Tip 2

Never use a resume or fill out an application. Since I can't spell or write very good, it would be kind of a waste of time anyway. And furthermore, a resume or application is nothing but a lying sheet. When someone tells you *we don't have an opening*, what they are really telling you is we have been looking for you for years and all you have to do is let them know you are the one for the job. Resumes and applications just confuse the issue. I can claim to be a brain surgeon on a piece of paper, but it doesn't mean I know how to cook eggs or wash dishes. If they hand you an application, hand it back and ask them to fill it out for you. Tell them that you can't write or read! That way they can't get you for lying on an application.

Secret Job-Hunting Tip 3

Well-worn clothes, shoes and week-old underwear are good. They will feel sorry for you and pity is a good thing when seeking a job.

Secret Job-Hunting Tip 4

Always carry a rolled up $20 bill in the palm of your hand when you shake hands with the interviewer and learn to pass it to them without being noticed. If they hand it back to ya, be prepared by pulling out a small Bible from your hip-pocket and hand it to them saying, "You are a good person, Brother" (or Sister whichever the case may be). In fact, if you are not sure what their name is, using the title of Brother or Sister always works well. You can never go wrong. Oh, it doesn't hurt to slip a $20 bill in the Bible as a bookmark! Think of it as a long-term investment. If they don't hire you, go over their head and inform their boss about them taking bribes. That'll get the ball rolling.

Secret Job-Hunting Tip 5

Scratching your armpits and picking your nose is fully acceptable. They will realize that you are just a good ole' Joe (or Jane) and that you are not trying to put on any airs, being totally yourself. When they call your name from a crowded waiting room, eye out the most likely person to be more qualified than you for the job, and stumble over their feet and scream loudly "You tripped me!" This is a great way to start out the interview, the potential employer feeling sorry for you while at the same time having bad thoughts about that tripper.

Secret Job-Hunting Tip 6

When you meet the interviewer, state clearly and plainly, "I am here for the job. I can read up to a 5th grade level, only drink on weekends, and I've never been addicted to any major drugs. I have been married seven times, I've got five starving kids to feed, and I haven't drawn welfare in the last thirty days. I am a working man and I can whup, with one hand tied behind my back, any one of them wimps sitting in the waiting room, Brother" (or Sister whichever the case may be). "Plus, I have no ambition at all so you will never have to worry about me climbing up the ladder and taking your job!" Before the interviewer has a chance to interrupt, ask clearly and plainly, "Would it be okay if I tour the building now?"

Secret Job-Hunting Tip 7

When touring the building, keep a close lookout for potential troublesome coworkers. Ideally, you would go to the interview with a cold or virus and do all you can to pass it on to the potential troublesome coworkers that may cause problems during your 90-

day trial. Also, if you get close enough to someone who looks like a troublesome coworker, trip in front of them and say, "Hey, you tripped me!" With a little practice, you will be able to sneeze on them while passing by.

Secret Job-Hunting Tip 8

The way you fill out the application makes all the difference in the world. Remember, never fill it out yourself. Have the interviewer or their assistant fill it out for you. Never put your own social security number or driver's license number on the application. It creates a hassle at tax time. Ideally, use your second or third ex-spouses' numbers, provided they can pass the background check. Always begin your title with "Brother" or "Sister", such as Brother Max Fetterbrush. Sounds more professional and has a biblical quality. And remember; never fill out the application yourself. Have someone else do it for you (even if you can write)! Having the statement available, "I can't help he (or she) put the wrong numbers down!" is a good thing. Yes, blameless deniability is golden!

Secret Job-Hunting Tip 9

Days before the interview, find out as many secrets as you can about the interviewer. Talk to ex-friends and ex-family members to get the best trash on them. If you are lucky enough to see them running around with some stranger of the opposite sex over the weekend, prior to the meeting, this will help on your interview date. Casually mention you saw them with their wife or husband and comment on how young they looked. Beyond affairs, any good garbage that might cause them to lose their job would be helpful, if carefully used. Just don't be pushy and don't be too obvious. Having photos available is good, too!

Secret Job-Hunting Tip 10

On the day of the interview, it would be excellent to consume a pot of well-cooked soup beans. Canned baked beans can work too if you eat enough of them. Here's how it works. You're waiting in line or in a waiting room to be interviewed and there are several waiting in line in front of you. If you can work the sickening farts just right, some of the others waiting to be interviewed may actually let you go in front of them to get you out of the room. You can even ask if they will let you go ahead of them, explaining your upset stomach and all. When the interviewer opens the door, and starts whiffing the air, just stare at the person behind you and say, "Whew; What did you eat for breakfast, Sister" (or Brother), and then pretend to be tripped by them. You might suggest that one of them people in line must have the stomach flu or something. This technique can get you hired on the spot so the interviewer doesn't have to be exposed to that sickly person. Just be sure and don't let one rip off while you're being interviewed.

Secret Job-Hunting Tip 11

When in the interviewer's office, look around the room for objects such as race car posters or anything that the interviewer finds valuable, and always start the interview by suggesting how well you love what they seem to love. If there is a picture of the company's president, state clearly and plainly, "That's my uncle/aunt, twice removed on my Mama's side. I didn't know he/she worked here. He (or she) was always my Mama's favorite brother (or sister). He was at Mama's funeral; God rest her soul."

Secret Job-Hunting Tip 12

When the interview seems to be close to ending, try to get the interviewer to lock you in a date and time to show up for work. If you've done your homework, you will know that they are race fans, (or opera fans) and you will have two pit passes (or balcony seats) to the next race (or opera), and you will hand them to them and say, "Here are some tickets to the race," (in which you have also placed five twenty-dollar bills in the middle). Say, "May God Bless!" Call the interviewer the next day and ask them if they are enjoying their money and if they see Uncle Prez, tell them to tell him that you said "Hello!" Ask, "When do I need to come to work?" Keep calling every day until they let you know! If this doesn't land you your job, go over their head and inform their boss about how they are extorting money and gifts from job seekers. Then call the nightly news whistleblowers hotline and the local newspaper and inform them about how badly this company treated you, anonymously of course. Now, you might as well go fishing!

The End!

If you liked Max, be sure and get your copy of the second volume in this series called *"Max Does America"*. Max up and takes off on his new ped to see America. You will go with Max across the backroads as he finds true love, a lot of money, new friends, and a crazy cat called Satan. If you laughed reading this book, you'll crack up when you start your journey with Max across America. Get your copy of *"Max Does America"* today.